Hob Tales

Book one

The Hob

and the

Deerman

Pat Walsh

Chapter One

The hob stood by the entrance to his burrow and sniffed the air. The autumn breeze ruffled his fur with its chilly fingers, making him shiver. Dusk was settling and a few early stars glimmered in the darkening sky above the forest. The old oak tree, amongst whose roots his burrow lay, spoke tree words into his mind. *A storm is coming, little hob. Stay close in your burrow this night.*

The hob patted the tree's gnarled trunk. 'We have weathered storms before, tree, many a time. There is no need to worry about this one.'

The breeze swayed through the gold and scarlet leaves of the forest trees, sighing and whispering, spreading word of the great wind coming this way.

The hob stepped inside his burrow and closed the door of closely woven hazel withies behind him. A tunnel wound its way down into the earth to his home amongst the roots of the oak tree. It was warm and comfortable and the hob looked around with a contented sigh. Whatever happened in the world above, he was safe here.

The treasures he had collected over the years stood on shelves made from fallen branches wedged between the roots: arrowheads made from golden flint, beads of amber and jet, a small iron buckle, coins of bronze and silver. A clay lamp held a flickering fay light, a small white flame which burned cold and never went out. Holey stones and feathers hung from the roots overhead, and swayed gently as he passed beneath them. His food store was a cupboard made from a carved wooden box, standing on end, its lid propped open. Shelves held baskets of berries and hazelnuts, dried brown mushrooms and crab apples, and a honeycomb he had found in a fallen tree; it smelled of bees and flowers and glowed like burnished gold in the lamplight.

The hob settled in his nest of moss and old leaves. For a while he lay and listened to the sound of the strengthening wind, muffled by the earth walls of his burrow, but sleep was close and dreams gathered in the corners of his mind.

He woke with a start when a shudder went through the tree. He pushed aside the moss and sat up.

The wind is strong and I am old, my friend. The tree words sounded inside the hob's head. *This night will not end well.*

The hob felt the tree's fear. He had never known the oak to be worried by a storm before. 'It will be over soon,' he whispered anxiously. 'Do not be frightened, tree.'

But the tree would not be reassured. Its roots clung more tightly to the earth as the storm wind grew stronger. The door of the burrow rattled and high overhead, the oak's great branches creaked and swayed. The hob cowered in his nest, his arms crossed over his

2

head. Around and above him, the roots of the ancient oak tree shifted. His treasures fell from the shelves and the holey stones clinked and jangled. The hob chittered in terror as stones and loose earth rattled down on him. Outside, the storm raged through the forest like a dragon.

'I do not like this,' he whimpered. 'Hold fast to the earth, tree!'

He felt a shudder go through the oak's roots; fear was raw in the dusty air. The wind whipped open the door of his burrow and stormed its way inside, tearing the hob's nest of moss and feathers to shreds in its icy jaws and sending him tumbling across the floor.

'Go away! *Go away!*' the hob shouted. He crouched into a tight huddle as the world collapsed around him. There was an almighty screech of splintering wood as the oak's roots were ripped from the forest floor. The ground beneath the hob's feet heaved and sent him tumbling heels over head into a corner of his burrow. Rain lashed down, quickly soaking his fur. Above the noise of the storm he heard the rending and smashing of branches as the oak fell, and the tree's spirit screamed in anguish.

From beneath his arms, the hob peered around in horror. High above him, the oak's roots were black scratches against the storm clouds. Where the oak had spread its branches, there was now a gaping wound in the forest canopy.

The hob crawled out of the wreckage of his burrow and knelt beside the fallen tree, stricken with grief for his fallen friend. The oak's distress was so great it swamped the hob's mind and for a while, the spirits of the hob and the tree were one.

The hob huddled beside the old oak through the long night. He talked to it and sang songs of the forest and of the animals, fays and humans who lived and hunted and sheltered there.

As the night passed, the storm blew itself out. Stars shone through ragged gaps in the clouds and at last, the hob felt the tree's spirit grow calm. A sense of peace finally settled over it and in doing so, a little of the hob's pain eased. Whatever bound the oak spirit to the dying tree gradually weakened until, as the grey dawn light spread across the eastern sky, it was finally set free. A glimmer of green light flickered between the branches and roots and the oak's voice whispered inside the hob's head: *Goodbye, my friend. Travel safely.*

The hob blinked away tears and nodded. 'You too, tree.'

The light swirled away through the clearing and up into the sky. Around him, the hob felt the sorrow of the other trees: a wild keen of mourning carried on the wind. The hob hunched his shoulders. The old oak's passing hurt him in a way he could find no words for. Grief was a splinter in his heart.

Shivering and sneezing, the hob got to his feet to inspect the state of his burrow. The walls had collapsed in a muddy landslide, mixed with broken branches and torn roots. All of his possessions and

4

his winter food store lay buried beneath it. There was nothing left to salvage.

I need to find shelter, he thought anxiously, *but it will take time to find a new tree and dig a burrow.*

He sneezed again and his stomach rumbled. Cold and hunger were no friends to a hob.

Where can I go? He crouched beside the ruin of his burrow, now just a deep muddy pool. Autumn was pulling on its winter coat and the days were shortening and growing colder. He needed to find somewhere soon, before the frosts came.

A memory stirred in the corner of the hob's mind, of winters and summers spent at the stone walled abbey beside the river. He had made his home there once and perhaps he could do so again, though he knew it would not be the same; the people he had known were long since dead and buried. With a surge of fondness, the hob remembered the small humpbacked monk, Brother Snail, the healer who made possets and salves, and tended to cuts and broken bones. After the monk died, all the hob had wanted to do was come home to Foxwist, to his burrow beneath the oak tree. And here he would have stayed if the oak had not been uprooted in the storm. *Perhaps I could go back to the abbey,* the hob thought hopefully as he rubbed his arms to try and warm himself, *just until the spring, when I can dig a new burrow. Maybe the stone buildings are no longer there but if they are, then perhaps I will find someone who might like to make the acquaintance of a homeless hob.*

The hob nodded to himself, his mind made up. *That is what I will do. I will go and see if the snail brother's hut is still there.*

With a last sorrowful look at the oak tree, now just dying timber, he wiped the rainwater drips from the fur around his eyes and set off to find the abbey.

Trusting his instincts, which often turned his feet in the right direction when his head did not know where to go, he followed barely-there paths through the forest, worn by foxes and fays over many years, until they narrowed and gradually dwindled away to nothing.

'I am not lost,' he said, looking around at unfamiliar trees. His voice sounded small in the damp autumn silence, 'even if I don't know where I am at this exact moment.'

The hob thought for a while. He was sure the abbey and the river were to be found on the edge of the forest, in the direction of the setting sun. He turned to get his bearings and then set off again. The storm had littered the forest with broken branches, making his journey slow. He was footsore and weary when at last he emerged from the trees onto a wide track full of deep ruts and puddles. For a few moments he gazed around. *I know this place!* he thought with a rush of relief. Beyond a ditch on the far side of the track, flood meadows led down a river. It had broken its banks and brown water nudged a tide line of flotsam between the reed beds and up onto the grassy slopes of the field.

If he followed the track one way he would reach the fording place across the Sheep Brook. The abbey stood across the river in the other direction. With a lift of his spirits, the hob set off towards it, sidestepping fallen branches and keeping a watchful eye open for puddles hidden by the last of the autumn leaves. Up ahead, on the far side of the river, he could see the grey stone walls of the abbey. There were more buildings than he remembered and a new timber bridge had taken the place of the old one. A new wall had been built on the bank above the river. It hid the gardens from any hobs who might be watching from the edge of the forest.

It was several moments before he realised that something was wrong: there was no smoke from the chimneys, no brother men coming and going along the causeway, no bells ringing.

A rumbling came from somewhere back along the track. The hob scurried back to the edge of the forest and climbed up to sit on a branch of a young oak tree. He watched two horse drawn carts creak and lurch through the muddy ruts below him. Two men sat on the seat board of the first cart, bundled in coats, hats and scarves against the damp chill of the autumn morning. A man and a boy, just as warmly dressed, travelled on the second cart.

'Well, I tell ye agin,' a man with a bristling black beard grumbled, 'I'm not stayin' at the abbey past dusk, and I don't care what the new lord of the manor has to say on it. I *ain't* stayin'. Not after what Jack Thatcher seen.'

His companion, a young sandy-haired man with pock-marked cheeks, snorted. 'Brave words, Tobias, but I'd pay me last penny to see ye say that to 'is lordship's face.'

The carter muttered something which the hob did not catch, but he could see the hunch of the man's shoulders and the scowling brow beneath the upturned brim of his woollen hat.

The hob peered into the cart as it passed by. Hammers, chisels and ropes lay beside piles of empty sacks and baskets. The horse pulling the cart turned its head and rolled a white-rimmed eye in his direction. Men could rarely see him, the hob knew, but animals could.

'See, even ol' Sampson don't want to be here,' Tobias the carter said, nodding to the horse's large rump. He lowered his voice and added, 'Scoff all ye like, Kit, but they say animals can *feel* ghosts, and that old abbey is full of 'em, if only half the tales told round here's true.'

The hob wrapped his tail around his body. *Ghosts?* he thought uneasily. A demon had walked the passageways and rooms of the abbey a long time ago, but the demon was dead. He did not remember any *ghosts*.

The carts trundled on past his hiding place. The hob's ears twitched as he listened to the carter's voice fading into the distance, still grumbling about ghosts.

The hob waited until they were a good way down the track before setting off after them, jumping over the ruts and fallen branches, lifting his tail clear of the puddles. By the time he reached the turning to the abbey, the carts had reached the bridge over the river. A dark-haired boy ran ahead to open the abbey gates. The hob watched with a puzzled frown. Where were the brother men? Why didn't one of *them* open the gates?

The carts passed beneath the gatehouse and rumbled away across the yard. The hob followed, running along the causeway as quickly as he could. He was worried that someone would close the gates before he could reach them but to his surprise nobody did. The carts were out of sight and the gatehouse passage was deserted. *How strange*, the hob thought as he hurried across the bridge. *When I lived here, the brother men never left them open like this. They kept the abbey things in and everything else out.*

The hob peered around the corner of the gatehouse. The carts had stopped outside the great West Door of the church and the men and the boy were climbing down onto the cobbles. Around them, the abbey buildings seemed unnaturally quiet. It struck the hob as odd that nobody had come to meet the carters. Where were the brother men?

A pigeon, disturbed by the carters' voices, clapped away across the yard. Startled, the hob glanced up and he gasped in shock as he saw that the roof and tower of the church were no longer there. All the coloured glass had gone from the windows and only the sky showed through the highest ones now.

Looking around, the hob noticed other things: the weeds growing between the yard cobbles, the gap where the small barn had once stood, the remains of a bonfire in the middle of the yard. Brambles and nettles grew wild in the empty pig and goat pens, and the large barn had lost one end of its roof thatch.

The hob shook his head and whispered, 'This is bad, very bad. Why have the brother men let this happen to their abbey?'

The hob watched as the men unloaded tools from the backs of the carts and carried them up the steps and into the church. The boy unharnessed the horses and led them over to the pasture behind the small barn.

The hob's heart leaped in his chest when a soft voice behind him asked, 'Who're *ye*?'

Startled, he spun on his heel and flattened himself against the gatehouse wall. A girl stood a few paces away, staring at him in wonder. She was as thin as a bundle of sticks, with hair the copper red of hens' feathers. Her pale skin was freckled like a sparrow's egg, but there were dark shadows beneath her eyes. The grubby blue dress she wore looked too flimsy to keep out the damp autumn chill. But she was no ordinary girl, the hob realised with a quiver of fear; he could see through her, as if her body was made of nothing more than river mist.

10

'Can't ye talk?' She sounded disappointed.

Just for a moment, the hob was tempted to turn and scurry away but something about the girl's eyes made him hesitate. The deep loneliness he glimpsed there stirred his pity. Cautiously, he nodded.

'Ye can?' the girl said eagerly. She smiled and knelt down on the cobbles, her dress pooling around her legs. 'I ain't seen ye here afore, but I know what ye are.'

The hob watched her warily. 'You do?'

The girl nodded. 'Thought ye were a big cat first off, with them big pointy ears and that hairy tail, but ye ain't, ye're a *fay*. So, what ye called?'

The hob merely stared at her. Was this strange spirit girl trying to trap him into telling her his name?

Perhaps she saw his look of suspicion because she laughed and shook her head. 'I forgot! Ye *can't* tell me, can ye? A fay's got to keep its name *secret*.'

The hob hesitated for a few moments, but he had the feeling that he could trust her. 'I have two names,' he said at last. 'You can call me Brother Walter.'

The girl looked impressed. '*Brother* Walter! Didn't know fay creatures could be *monks*.'

'I don't think they can,' the hob said. 'One of the brother men gave me that name a long time ago. He was my friend,' he added softly, remembering the first time he had met Brother Snail.

11

The girl touched her chest with thin, dirty fingers. 'Well, I'm Johanna Gaudy. I got two names an' all, and ye can call me Urchin.'

The name was familiar. The hob's brow wrinkled as he tried to recall where he had heard it before. *That is what the snail brother used to call hedgepigs,* he thought. 'That's a strange name for a human.'

A look of sadness crossed her face and tears gleamed in her eyes. ''S what my father calls me.'

'Why?' the hob asked.

The girl shrugged. 'He just does.'

'Where is he?' he asked.

Urchin blurred and faded until she was just a shimmer of blue and red against the grey stones of the gatehouse wall. The hob watched in alarm. It was unsettling to see someone disappear like that in front of your eyes.

'I ain't seen him for the longest time, not since I fell sick at the Cold Fair in Yagleah and he fetched me here.' Urchin's voice was soft as falling leaves and she sounded as if she was crying. 'He said he would come back for me, but he didn't. Every year when the frost starts to bite I try to go and look for him but I can't leave the abbey, it won't let me go. And now the fair's 'bout to start again, and he'll be waitin' but I won't be there...'

And with that, she was gone, though her unhappiness lingered on like a dark cloud. The hob sat there for a while, just in case she

12

reappeared, but she did not. Between the ghost girl and the ruined buildings, he was beginning to wonder if coming back to the abbey had been such a good idea after all.

Chapter Two

The sound of hammering, the hollow chink of metal on stone, came from the church. The hob was curious to see what the men were doing, but something tugged at his heart and his memory. *I need to find the snail brother's hut, to see if any whisper of him is still there. I need to find my old friend.*

The abbey would not be the same without Brother Snail's gentle and kindly presence, but then Urchin's spirit was still here, so perhaps the monk had not left either. *I will tell him about my oak tree and he will listen and understand, and the world will not feel so strange.*

The hob hurried across the yard to the animal pens, now lost in a lake of nettles. A path led past the pens to the abbey gardens. The wattle gate had been pulled from its hinges and it lay on the ground, grown through with bindweed and grass. Beyond it, the gravel path had narrowed to a fox track between beds of weeds. The vegetable garden was a wilderness, and the orchard was neglected and littered with broken branches and rotting brown fruit. In his mind the hob saw carefully tended beds with rows of herbs and vegetables, and brother men harvesting apples on late summer days. All gone and forgotten now.

The hob followed the path to Brother Snail's hut and stared around in dismay. The old wooden hut and its sheltering blackthorn

14

tree had gone. In their place, an unfamiliar stone building stood amongst the brambles and long grass. The charred roof timbers and soot-streaked walls told their own story.

'Are you still here?' he asked hopefully, but there were no words of welcome, no sense of the snail brother's presence in the misty stillness of the abandoned garden.

With a heavy sigh, the hob sat on the path. For the first time in his long life, he felt old and tired. Loneliness was a heavy weight on his shoulders. *I would like for us to sit by the fire where we could talk about hob things and man things, just as we used to,* he thought, seeing the snail brother's smiling face in his mind.

The hob slowly retraced his steps through the lost garden. When he reached the gateway to the yard, he stood for a while and wondered what to do now. He picked up a flat little pebble and licked one side. It tasted of earth and the faint tang of footsteps that had long since walked by.

'Dry side up and I will go back to the forest, licked side up and I will stay here tonight,' he said, flicking his paw to send the pebble spinning through the air. It landed on the cobbles by his feet, licked side up. The choice was made. *I will stay for now, and if I am to stay, then I want to see what the men are doing in the church.*

The hob ran across the yard and up the steps to the great West Door of the church, and peered inside. The men were nowhere to be seen but the sound of voices and hammering came from the north transept. He set off along the south aisle and hid behind a nave pillar. From here he saw that the church was open to the sky and filled with grey daylight. A blackened and charred pile of timber lay on the floor amongst scatters of broken stone, plaster and weeds. Unburned fragments showed that the wood had been carved and painted. One piece, dark blue with tiny golden stars, lay in a puddle near the pillar, like a patch of midnight sky that had fallen to earth. He reached out a paw and picked it up before gently wiping away the muddy water. The edges of the wood were burned and there was a deep gouge where it had been hit with an axe. The hob stroked the stars and wondered why anyone would destroy such a beautiful thing. Holding the wood close to his chest, he stared at the scene of ruin around him.

From his hiding place behind the pillar, he could see that most of the north transept had gone. The walls were just stumps of rubble core, standing no higher than a full-grown man. All the worked stone was gone. A scaffold of wooden poles, ladders and planks stood against the last bit of wall where it turned the corner into the nave. At the top of the scaffold, the sandy-haired man and an older man with grey-streaked dark hair hacked at the painted plaster with chisels and hammers, sending it showering down, the saints and angels lost forever as they shattered into countless fragments on the tiled floor. The boy carried a wicker basket full of rubble to a handcart in the nave, while the dark-bearded man, Tobias, stacked blocks of stone onto a second cart.

The hob chittered softly in agitation as he watched the men dismantle the ancient wall, stone by stone. He left the church and climbed onto the back of one of the wattle-sided carts where he settled behind a stack of empty baskets to brood on what was happening at the abbey. By now he was sure that the monks no longer lived here. Did they know what was happening to their old home? If they did not come back soon, there would be nothing to come back to.

He propped the piece of painted wood against the side of the cart. It was like looking out at a night sky full of stars through a small window.

There was a basket of tools on the cart. The hob frowned at the battered wooden handles, the nicked and dull chisel blades, all caked with dried mortar and mud. He clicked his tongue crossly and looked around for something he could use to clean them. He found a leather water bottle, a whetstone and a jar of beeswax in a leather bag, along with some old linen rags.

He set about honing the chisel blades, and cleaning and waxing the handles, and then started on the hammers and mallets. He was so absorbed in his work that at first he did not notice the dark-haired boy standing at the back of the cart.

'What...?' The boy's eyes were the colour of newly turned earth and they widened in astonishment when he saw the gleaming, polished tools. He picked up a chisel and turned it over in his hands, then ran a careful finger along the sharpened blade.

17

He shook his head slowly. 'Well, I'll be...'

The hob sat perfectly still, the woollen waxing rag held tightly in his paw. Was it his imagination, or did the boy's gaze flicker towards him and linger there for just a moment?

The boy quickly covered the tools with a sack and took an earthenware jug and a wicker basket from the cart. The hob sniffed hungrily; he could smell food, and by the malty tang of it, the jug held beer. It was a long time since he had smelled *that*.

The three men came out of the church, slapping stone and plaster dust from their clothes and hair.

'Make yerself useful, Ned,' the man with the greying dark hair said as he took the jug from the boy's hands, 'light a fire in the barn. There's a bite in the air today so we might as well be warm while we eat.'

'I will, Father, soon as I find the tinderbox,' Ned said.

The two other men fetched jugs and baskets from their own cart and walked across the yard towards the large barn.

Ned waited until the men were out of earshot. 'Thank ye for yer help,' he said softly. A flush rose to his cheeks and his nervous gaze flicked over the cart, as if he did not dare to look directly at the hob. With shaking fingers, he took a loaf of bread from the basket and broke off a piece. Taking a small knife from his belt, he cut a thick slice from a wedge of cheese, and took two small red apples from the basket. He laid the food on the corner of a sack and turned to go, but

18

then hesitated. 'I'll have to let my father think I cleaned the tools,' Ned said, an apologetic note in his voice. 'Don't be offended, it's just...he ain't going to believe me if I tell him who *really* done the work.'

The hob understood. It was the usual way of things in his dealings with humans. Some knew him for what he was and accepted him, but most people did not.

Glancing at him for the first time, the boy swallowed and cleared his throat nervously and his cheeks lost a little of their colour. 'How come I ain't seen ye afore now? Ye been hiding from us?'

'I came here from the forest this morning,' the hob said, 'after my burrow was destroyed in the storm.'

Ned nodded. 'Ay, it was a bad one.'

The hob glanced around at the deserted abbey and felt a dusting of sadness settle over him. 'But I used to live here, long, *long* ago. I came back because I have nowhere else to go until the spring, when I can dig a new burrow in the forest.'

'Ye lived with the monks?' Ned asked, looking surprised. 'Didn't know they felt kindly towards creatures such as yerself.'

'They don't usually,' the hob said. 'But one of them was my friend.'

Ned glanced around at the abbey buildings, then pulled a face. 'I suppose it ain't the same as ye remember, then.'

The hob shook his head. 'Not the same at all.'

'Well, I'd best go, afore my father comes looking for his food,' Ned said. 'Maybe I'll see ye again.' With a quick nod, he hurried away, clutching the basket.

Well, this is a nice surprise, the hob thought as he inspected the pile of food the boy had shared with him. He bit into the crumbly white cheese. It tasted sharp and goaty. *I like the boy. He knows how to talk to a hob; he appreciates a hob.*

The bread was crusty and freshly baked and the apples held all the sweetness of warm summer days. He saved the pips and core for last and crunched them contentedly. When his belly was full, he felt ready for a nap. He peered over the side of the cart. Ned and the men were still inside the barn. Threads of smoke rose up through holes in the thatched roof.

The hob tucked the painted wood panel beneath his arm and climbed down from the cart, knowing he needed to find somewhere safe to make a new nest. The barn seemed the most promising place but he would have to wait until the men had gone back to work in the church. He would find somewhere else for now. Looking around, he remembered the pigpen where he had wiled away many a happy afternoon in the company of his old friend, the abbey's spotted sow. She was long gone now, of course, but visiting the pen would bring back good memories.

The hob crossed the yard and pushed his way through the brittle dead stalks of nettles growing around the pen. His thick fur

20

protected him from thorns as he crawled beneath brambles to the open-fronted stone shelter. Part of the roof had collapsed but a few timbers still covered one corner and the hob settled there. He propped the wooden sky with its golden stars against the wall and gazed at it for a while. *It's my own piece of night,* he thought sleepily. *I can keep my dreams there when I am not thinking them.*

The hob had just begun to doze when something nudged his leg. He sat up in fright and stared around, but the pen was empty. The hob watched and waited; sometimes hidden things were shy and took time to show themselves. The hob closed his eyes again. This time, the nudge was more insistent, and he smelled warm pig. He grinned with delight as he reached out and felt a solid body. All the long years since he had last seen Mary Magdalene just melted away as, with a contented grunt, she settled down beside him. The hob opened one eye but there was still nothing to see so he closed it again; fay magic let her body feel warm and real to him and he was satisfied with that. He scratched her behind the ear and rubbed her bristly back and she grunted happily. He curled up against her flank and fell asleep.

Chapter Three

The hob woke to the sound of cartwheels grating on the cobbles. The day was fading into dusk and he realised he had slept the afternoon away. The pig had gone and he was alone. He crawled under the brambles and peered through a gap in the fence, just in time to see the carts trundling along the passageway beneath the gatehouse, loaded with stone blocks. When the carts reached the causeway, Ned ran back to close the gates and silence settled over the abbey.

The rainclouds had cleared and the sky was palest blue. The buildings along one side of the yard were burnished to soft gold by the setting sun, while shadows settled in the lee of the barn and gatehouse. Cawing rooks flew in ragged groups towards their winter roost in the forest.

The hob rubbed his arms, warming himself against the early evening chill. The atmosphere in the yard had subtly changed with the dying of the day. Without Ned or the old pig for company, it felt very lonely. In his memories, the abbey was busy with monks going about their daily chores, chickens in the yard, sheep bleating in the fields, bells ringing, cooking smells drifting from the kitchen. He did not know *this* abbey, this silent and abandoned place.

The hob took the painted wooden sky from the corner of the pigpen and set off across the yard towards the barn, where he could make himself a nest. A row of flat stones ran through the cobbles.

22

They made a line from the buildings on the south side of the cloister, across the yard and down towards the river. The hob stopped by a dark hole where several of the stones were missing, and listened. He could hear running water. A memory stirred at the back of his mind; the stones covered a drain, through which the brother men had channelled a stream. It carried the waste from their latrines down to the river.

A shuffling sound came from the drain, as if something was creeping along it, towards the hole. *A rat?* the hob wondered. It sounded too large for that. Claws scratched on stone and a ripe, gamey smell caught in the back of the hob's throat and made him cough.

That is disgusting! The hob clapped a paw over his nose and mouth and took a hurried step back. *That is not a rat smell; it is something much worse and I know what it is.* Hundreds of years of instinctive fear pushed a word to the front of his mind and sent panic surging through him: *boggart*. Nothing else smelled quite that bad, and it was the only fay creature he could think of who would choose to live in a drain.

And then he saw two eyes, gleaming deep crimson, watching him from the darkness. The hob leaped back in terror as a long, thin arm shot out and clawed fingers snatched at his leg, ripping out tufts of fur. He just managed to scramble away before the boggart tried again.

Clutching the painted wood to his chest, the hob looked around in terror and saw an open door at the corner of the south range, leading to the abbey kitchen. He fled for the safety of its stone walls, desperate to outrun the creature and find somewhere safe to hide. Claws clattered on the cobbles close behind him. He pushed up the door latch and threw himself across the threshold. He glimpsed a dark hunched shape loping towards him and quickly slammed the door. He stared wildly around the kitchen. The chamber was as gloomy as a cave, empty of everything except shadows and a creeping damp that streaked the walls. Dead leaves had blown down the chimney of the huge brick fireplace and lay scattered across the floor. Bird droppings formed chalky piles on the hearth and below the roof beams. Tiny bundles of fur and small bones told him that owls roosted here. There was nowhere to hide and he could hear the boggart on the other side of the door, sniffing and grunting and rattling the latch.

On the far side of the kitchen, the door to the cloister stood ajar. The hob hurried into the south alley and stood for a few moments, wondering where to go. The cloister was a passageway, open on one side, around the edge of a square, wildly overgrown garden. He could see doors set into the walls, leading to dimly remembered rooms, but there was no time to search for a safe place to hide.

'Quick, liddle fay! This way!'

The hob squeaked in fright, but to his relief, he saw Urchin, her face moon pale in the deepening dusk, standing by an arched opening at the far end of the south alley. She pointed to the flight of stone steps leading up to the monks' dorter.

'Hurry! Don't let the demon catch ye!'

'It's a boggart,' the hob said breathlessly as he ran towards her.

Urchin faded and disappeared. A moment later, her voice drifted down the dark staircase. 'Up here, Brother Walter!'

The hob scurried though the archway and up the narrow steps. Urchin was waiting for him in the long room at the top. She pointed to the roof. 'Hide there. The demon ain't good at climbin'.'

'Boggart,' the hob wheezed.

Most of the roof tiles were missing. Through the web of rafters, he saw the waxing moon. A beam had fallen from the roof and leaned against the wall. The hob climbed it as quickly as he could while still holding the painted wood. Looking down, he saw that Urchin had vanished again. He could hear the boggart snuffling in the cloister alley as it cast about to catch his scent, and then he heard the click of claws on the stairs.

The hob crept along a rafter to hide in the darkness beneath a few remaining roof tiles. He held the painted stars tightly and made himself as small as he could.

It was too dark to see the boggart clearly, but he saw enough to tell him that the creature was easily twice his size and covered in shaggy black fur. Away from the shelter of the drain, it smelled stomach-curdlingly bad. It stood in the middle of the room, sniffing, and then suddenly went silent. It looked up and its red eyes glowed like embers as it stared at the hob's hiding place.

It can smell me, the hob realised fearfully. There was no point trying to hide; the creature did not rely on sight to find what it was looking for, it simply sniffed it out. The hob huddled into a tighter ball and breathed as gently as he could.

The boggart grunted and huffed as it slapped the floor, its claws clacking against the wooden boards. It flung a thin arm wide and jabbed a claw towards the staircase. The grunts grew louder and the creature seemed agitated. The hob watched in terror as it dug its claws into one of the timber beams and started to edge its way up. Urchin was only partly right; the creature was not good at climbing but that did not mean it could not climb at all. It slowly edged its way towards him, grunting and snuffling with the effort.

The hob was panic-stricken. He had no doubt that this would not end well if the boggart caught him; it would not be particular about what it ate, and a hob was as good as a frog or a rat. He peered out through the hole in the roof, looking for a way to escape, but he was too high up and there was no way to get down to the cloister

26

without throwing himself to almost certain death on the roof of the east alley.

The boggart's head jerked sharply to one side and it stopped climbing. An odd shuffling sound came from the staircase and the hob felt a creeping chill in the air that slowly wrapped itself around his shivering body. The boggart made small guttural sounds and slithered back down the beam. It slunk over to the door where it peered down the stairway. Whatever was coming up, the boggart did not like it one little bit.

The sound stopped. The hob tensed, expecting the boggart to turn its attention back to him, but instead, the creature gave a low growl and shuffled back from the stairs.

The hob's fur bristled with fright. What had scared the boggart? He stared at the doorway, dreading what he would see. A shadow moved onto the landing. He knew something was there, watching him, as surely as he knew his own name.

Chapter Four

Evil seeped through the chamber like the darkness inside a nightmare. The boggart held its ground but the hob could see it crouching low and hear the growls rumbling in its chest.

The shadow on the landing moved and a hunched shape crawled into the dorter, trailing rags and a smell of decay. The hob whimpered in terror and clung to a rafter with shaking paws. The boggart's growls were louder now but it did not back away from the thing shuffling across the floor. It thumped the floorboards with its fist and gave a warning grunt.

'Go away, go *away*!' the hob whispered, but whether it was to the boggart or the tattered grey creature, he did not know. He gasped in fright as the thing lifted its head and turned blind white eyes towards him. Its face was a mask of dead flesh, dried out and withered, its blackened lips drawn back into a terrible grin. The boggart grunted again and pounded its fists on the floor. The creature's head jerked awkwardly on its neck and it turned its blind stare on the boggart.

The hob felt a bitter draught stir around him and the thing on the floor fade and twist away like smoke on the breeze. The feeling of evil lifted and the only sounds in the gathering darkness were the boggart's huffs. It gave the floor a final thump, then loped to the staircase and was gone.

28

It was a long time before the hob dared to move. The realisation that the ragged creature was not flesh and bone but something *other*, something darker, terrified him. The boggart's bravery surprised him; they were not known for their courage, but it had saved him from the crawling thing, whether it had intended to or not.

The hob climbed down from the rafters. He was as sure as he could be that the crawling thing had gone. He peered down the staircase but there was no sign of the boggart.

Moving silently on hairy feet, the hob crept down the stairs and looked cautiously along the cloister alley. It was too dark to see if anything was hiding there but his senses were sharp and he did not feel the tell-tale tingle between his shoulders to warn him that something was not right. But even so, the garden in the middle of the cloister was a well of dusky shadows, lit by the last glow of daylight. Eerie shapes seemed to form out of the twisted patterns of dark and light. Gathering what courage he could pull together, he ran back to the kitchen.

The yard door stood open, and the hob looked outside. The hole in the drain was a dark patch on the cobbles but the yard was empty. He ran as fast as he could to the barn and opened the door just wide enough to slip through. Things scurried in the darkness, but he smelled rat and mouse and spider and he was not frightened. He climbed the ladder to the hayloft and to his delight he found a pile of old dry hay in a corner, still holding the faintest scents of a long ago meadow. He shaped it into a nest and leaned the piece of starry wood against a nearby roof post. Settling himself on his back in the hay, he gazed up at the real stars through a hole in the roof. They were tiny and white, not like the golden ones on his wooden sky. Owls hunted in the forest across the river, hooting and screeching, a comfortingly familiar sound.

The barn's wooden walls made him feel safe. It brought to mind the snail brother's hut by the blackthorn tree. But even so, fear trembled through his body at the memory of the grey, dead thing and the evil that had oozed from it, like poison from a wound. He settled deeper into the straw but lay awake long into the night, his ears pricked for the sound of something creeping through the darkness towards his nest. His dreams, when he finally slept, were unsettling: a shadow shape followed him through roofless chambers and along dark passageways, and no matter how hard he tried to escape from it, his legs would not let him run. Leaden and slow, they barely moved, and the thing trailing him got steadily closer...

The hob woke with a jolt, heart thumping. For a moment, he could not untangle the dream from the cold grey dawn. Was the touch of that bony hand on his shoulder real? He sat up quickly and stared around, his eyes wide with terror. The hayloft was empty. He took a deep, unsteady breath. 'Just a dream,' he whispered. His paws were shaking as he pushed aside the straw and got to his feet. He was tired after his disturbed night but did not want to sleep again. The dream might be waiting for him, and he did not want to find out how it ended.

The hob climbed down the ladder and opened the barn door just wide enough to let in the early morning light. With his back against the wooden timbers of the door, he settled down to wait for Ned and the carts.

The hob inspected the pile of tools Ned had brought with him on the cart that morning.

'My father's Noll Swyfte, master carpenter in Yagleah,' Ned explained. He leaned his arms on the side of the cart and stared at the hob, openly curious now that he had got over his initial shock at coming across a fay creature. 'He makes new handles for old farm tools and kitchen knives and things, but since he's been working here at the abbey for Sir Samuel, he ain't had time to do this lot. I thought, as ye made such a good job of our chisels and hammers yesterday...?' He smiled hopefully and added, 'I'll share me food with ye.'

The hob lifted a sickle and frowned at the blunt blade. 'Hmm.'

'But I still have to let him think *I* done the work,' Ned said, his cheeks reddening. 'Not sure how he'll take it, knowing a hob's living at the abbey, and mending our tools.'

31

The hob gave him a hard stare. 'Very well, and in case you were wondering, I liked the goaty cheese. A piece of that would be fair reward for my help.'

Ned looked relieved. 'As much as ye want,' he said with a grin.

The hob nodded, satisfied with this arrangement. 'Who is Sir Samuel?'

'He lives in the old manor in Yagleah and owns half the land hereabouts, including the abbey and all its fields and sheep and vineyards. He bought it after King Henry closed all the abbeys and friaries and is using the stone to build himself a fine new house. That's what we're doing, taking stone from the church walls for the house.' He paused and the hob had the feeling that something was worrying the boy.

'And we been looking for carved stones too, 'cause he wants it to be the fairest house in these parts, but they're disappearing afore we can take 'em.'

'Somebody is stealing them?' the hob asked, baffled. Why would anyone steal stones, carved or otherwise?

Ned shook his head. 'Don't rightly know *what's* happening to 'em.'

'So the brother men aren't coming back, ever?' the hob asked.

'How can they?' Ned said. 'When there ain't any monks *anywhere*, not anymore.'

'Why? Where have they all gone?'

Ned shrugged. 'The king had 'em all turned out of the abbeys and other holy places when he closed 'em. Some're on the road, begging. Some's gone home to their families.' He paused for a moment, a troubled look on his face. 'Some are dead. Like the abbot of Crowfield.'

'What made him die?' the hob asked.

'Not *what*, but *who*,' Ned said. He picked at a loose bit of wood on the side of the cart, frowning. 'Abbot Matthew wouldn't tell the king's men where the abbey treasure was hid. They tortured him but it didn't do 'em no good, 'cause he never told 'em *anything*.' He looked over his shoulder and nodded to the gatehouse. 'Hanged him, they did, from the gate arch.'

The hob stared at him, horrified. 'The king must be a bad man to want treasure so badly he will kill people for it.'

'The killing of the abbot was nothing to do with the king. The leader of the men who came here to close the abbey were wicked to the bone, so people round here say. *He* was the one who gave the order to hang the abbot.' Ned's frown deepened and he gazed into the distance.

The king sounds greedy and just as wicked as his men, the hob thought darkly, *even if he did not tell anyone to hang Abbot Matthew.* 'Was the king angry with him for hanging the brother man and not bringing him the treasure?'

33

Ned would not meet his eyes. He forced a smile and stepped away from the cart. 'Who knows?'

The boy is hiding a secret, the hob thought, watching Ned closely. *There is more here than he is saying.*

'Sir Samuel's been looking for the treasure ever since he bought the abbey.' Ned said, with a gleam in his eye. 'But wherever the abbot hid it, he hid it well.'

'You do not like Sir Samuel?' he hob asked. It was there in the boy's voice.

'Nobody in Yagleah does.'

'Why?'

'First thing he did when he arrived in the village was to fence off the common land as pasture for his sheep. That's always been *our* land,' Ned said angrily. 'And then he pulled down four village houses 'cause he didn't want to see 'em from the windows of his new house.'

'What happened to the people inside?' the hob asked in concern.

'They piled all their belongings on carts and went to stay with relatives in the village, all squashed together like ducks in a basket.'

The hob shook his head slowly. 'That is not good.'

'No, it ain't.' Ned sighed and then asked, 'Have ye got a name?'

'Brother Walter.'

'*Brother?* Ye ain't a monk!' he said with a grin.

'Even so, that is what I am called.' The hob regarded the boy thoughtfully for a moment. 'You can see hobs, but you are not frightened. Why?'

Ned's eyebrows twitched upwards and he shrugged. 'Why should I be? I know about hobmen, from my mam's sister Bess. A hob lived in their father's house when they were girls, but only Bess could see it. She always said it were a *good* thing having a hob living with them. Knows all about hobs and fays does Bess. And anyhow, ye ain't dangerous.' He frowned at the hob. 'Are ye?'

The hob hunted for a whetstone. 'No.'

'Well, that's good then, ain't it.' Ned sounded relieved. 'Ye and me'll be good friends, I can tell.'

The hob set to work with the whetstone and the beeswax. Ned left him to it and went to help the men in the church.

'I'm right glad the crawlin' man didn't catch ye,' Urchin said. The hob looked up and saw her sitting on the cart seat, her red hair and blue dress vividly sharp in the clear morning air.

'Thank you,' he said, 'for showing me a safe place to hide. I don't know what would have happened if you hadn't helped me, but it would not have been good.'

'Ye're my friend, liddle Walter; I wouldn't let *anythin'* bad happen to ye.'

He looked around for something to give her, a small gift to show his deep gratitude for her friendship as well as her help. There

35

was an empty snail shell amongst the bits of stone and straw in a corner of the cart. It was marked with a spiral of pale yellow on the honey brown shell. The colours made him think of spring, of primroses growing up through last year's dead leaves. He put it on the seat beside her. 'For you.'

Her thin fingers passed through the shell but he heard the smile in her voice as she said, 'Thank ye, but ye will have to keep it safe for me.'

He picked up the shell and nodded. 'I will, I promise.'

A breeze stirred the air and she was no longer there. He put the shell back in the corner, out of harm's way, and carried on with his work.

Shortly before midday, two men on horseback rode through the gateway and over to the church. One was soberly dressed in a leather jerkin and trousers as brown as his sturdy mare. But it was the other man who caught and held the hob's attention, and the hob stared at him in astonishment. Short, fat and dressed in garish crimson clothes, the hob thought he looked like a large boil, ready to burst. A crimson and blue hat flopped over his lank fair hair and his bad-tempered face glistened with sweat in spite of the chilly autumn breeze. He wheezed as he struggled to dismount from his black gelding.

'Help me, can't you?' the man called peevishly. His companion rolled his eyes as he tied his mare's reins to the side of the cart where the hob was working. The hob ducked out of sight, but the man did not even glance in his direction.

'Hurry, man! We don't have all day.' The fat man scowled as his companion put a hand on his ample rump to steady him as he half slid, half jumped onto the cobbles.

'Swyfte!' he shouted, his voice sharp with impatience. 'Where are you, man?'

Ned's father came to the church door and frowned. 'Sir Samuel. I weren't expecting to see ye here today.'

'What you expect is of no interest to me,' Sir Samuel snapped. He waved a dimpled hand towards his companion, who was tying the gelding's reins to the cart beside the mare. 'My steward, Master Dunch, is here to inspect the carved stones for himself, as *you* plainly cannot be trusted to select the best ones.'

The hob saw Noll Swyfte's mouth harden into an angry line, but the carpenter said nothing. He merely stood aside to let Sir Samuel and Master Dunch go ahead of him into the church.

Full of curiosity, the hob climbed down from the cart and went after them. He hid behind a pillar in the south aisle. Tobias and Kit, up on the scaffold, stopped work to watch the lord of the manor as he walked slowly past a row of stones laid out on the nave floor, scowling. Master Dunch squatted beside a large column capital and ran a hand over the surface. Noll stood in silence, arms folded and a look of defiance in his eyes.

37

'I instructed you to collect up the *carved* stones,' Sir Samuel said, 'but these are all plain.'

'Ain't no decorated pieces from this part of the church,' Noll said evenly.

'Don't be so ridiculous, man! I saw them for myself at midsummer, at the top of the pillars. And there are plenty more in the chapter house and side chapels. So what have you done with them, eh? Did you break them, perhaps? And now you are trying to cover up your clumsiness?'

Anger burned in Noll's dark eyes. 'No!'

'Watch your tone with me, Swyfte.'

The hob held his breath. He felt the tension between the two men, building like a summer storm. Noll opened his mouth to speak, but in the same moment, Master Dunch straightened up and turned to Sir Samuel with a puzzled expression.

'This is most curious, your lordship,' he said.

'Hmm? What is?' Sir Samuel frowned at him.

'This capital,' the man said slowly. He pointed to a smooth, blank stone. 'I would have expected it to be carved but it is as if whatever was cut into the stone has simply...vanished.' He nodded to another capital. 'And it's the same with that one too.'

'I'm not interested in the stones they *didn't* carve, man,' Sir Samuel blustered. 'I just want you to find the ones they *did*!'

'But that is what I'm *telling* you, my lord. These stones should be decorated, all of them, but they are not and I cannot understand why.'

The hob saw the looks that went between the Yagleah men. They knew something about this, he was certain, but whatever it was, they were in no hurry to share it with Sir Samuel and his steward.

'You there, Swyfte,' Sir Samuel said, 'make it your business to find carved stones for my new house. They are here somewhere. Bring them to Yagleah Manor or I will find someone else to do it and you will not be paid a penny for your work, do you understand?'

Noll gave a brief nod. 'Yes, m'lord,' he muttered.

Without another word, Sir Samuel walked from the church.

Master Dunch waited until the lord of the manor was out of earshot before turning to Noll. He cleared his throat but did not look the carpenter in the eye. 'Perhaps my wits are softening to butter inside my head, but these stones were carved with birds and beasts the last time I saw them.'

'Ah...well.' Noll picked up a hammer and looked as if he wanted to be anywhere else at all but talking to the steward.

Master Dunch stared at Noll for a few moments longer, and then followed Sir Samuel out of the church.

Tobias Bodfish climbed down from the scaffolding and came to stand beside Noll. 'He ain't wrong though, is he? Last time we saw the stones, they were carved, and now they ain't.'

Noll glanced at the smooth stones at his feet. 'No. They ain't.'

'So what's happened to them, Noll?'

Noll Swyfte's face tightened into a frown. Without a word, he turned and walked away.

Chapter Five

'Brother Walter?'

The hob looked over the side of the cart and saw Ned standing nearby. The afternoon light was fading and the boy carried a lantern with a lit stub of tallow candle inside.

'My father told me to go and see how many carved stones are left in the cloister and chapter house. Ye can come and help me, if ye like.'

The boy does not need my help, the hob thought. *Perhaps he just does not want to be alone in this haunted place.* But he was happy to keep Ned company. He had spent the day cleaning and sharpening tools and now that the last of them was finished, he had nothing else to do.

The hob followed Ned into the church. The boy set off along the nave, the lantern flame flickering like a will o' the wisp in the gloom as he side-stepped the handcarts and the piles of stone and rubble. The hob scurried along the south aisle to the cloister door. For a few moments he stood in the doorway and sniffed the air. There was no tell-tale boggart smell, and nothing to hint that the crawly thing was close by. They should be safe enough for now. The arches opening onto the garden let the last of the daylight into the alleys and a cold breeze sent dead leaves skittering along the tiled floor. The hob watched Ned walk slowly along the north alley, head back as he looked up at the stone bosses decorating the ribs of the vaulted roof.

'Well, *this* ain't summat ye expect to find in a holy place,' Ned said. 'The Green Man.'

The hob saw a face with leafy branches growing out of its mouth and ears, painted in shades of green and brown, with scarlet holly berries amongst the leaves. 'No, he belongs in the forest and he does not look like *this*.'

Ned's eyebrows jerked upward in astonishment. 'Ye've *seen* it?'

'Many times, but it is made of green shadows and leaf ghosts. That,' he gave the roof boss a hard look, 'is a tree with a face.'

Ned walked on down the alley, holding up the lantern. 'A dog 'n' hare... an angel...fishes...and...ye!' He turned to the hob with a look of surprise. 'See? It's *ye!*'

The hob hurried over to look. The boss was hidden in the dark corner where the north and west alleys met. Ned was right; it looked very like him, from the tufted ears and small pointed face, to the long bristly tail. It held something tightly in one paw, as if it was frightened it might lose this small treasure, but the hob could not make out what it was supposed to be.

'Whoever carved it must have seen ye,' Ned said, 'when ye lived here.'

The hob shook his head. 'I have never seen it before. It must have been made after I went back to the forest.'

'Well, *someone* knew what a hob looked like,' Ned said. He walked on and turned the corner into the west alley.

The hob stayed where he was, staring up at the creature on the roof boss. It was like looking at his reflection in water, so alike were they. The hob had the oddest feeling that if he watched for long enough, he would see the stone eyes blink.

'Did you find any more carvings?' the hob asked when Ned returned.

The boy shook his head. His face was pale and he seemed tense. 'They're all gone.'

The hob climbed onto the stone bench running along the inner wall of the alley. Ned sat beside him, huddled inside his coat, and set the lantern on the floor by his feet.

'*All* gone?' the hob said, bewildered.

The boy nodded. 'Sir Samuel's stonemasons started working here at midsummer, taking down the walls. Then summat happened and they took off back to Yagleah and refused to come here again, so 'is lordship's payin' us to fetch the stone instead. When we started work at the end of August, just after St Bartholomew's day, the church was full of carvings and the walls were painted with saints and angels and the like, but they ain't here now. Every morning, we find more gone in the night, and the ones in the south transept weren't

43

there this morning.' He nodded to the roof bosses. 'This lot and a fistful of others are all that's left, unless there're still some in the chapter house.'

'Why did the stonemasons leave?' the hob asked, his voice sounding small in the cold stone stillness.

'They said the abbey was haunted but they wouldn't say what they saw. Then Jack Thatcher swore he saw a creature of rags and bones right here in the cloister, when he was relieving himself. Took off like a scalded pig, he did, and ran all the way back to Yagleah. That was a week ago and he says he ain't coming back here again, ever, not even if ye paid him in gold.' Ned stared back along the west alley, head to one side as he listened. He pulled a face and looked at the hob. 'Always think I hear things in here...don't like being in the cloister at all.'

The hob edged a little closer to the boy and glanced around anxiously. The lantern flame was very small in the darkening alley and the shadows were creeping closer. 'There *is* an evil spirit haunting the abbey.'

Ned stared at him, his eyes wide with fear. 'There really is? Ye've seen it for yerself?'

The hob nodded. 'In the brother men's sleeping place.'

The colour left Ned's face. 'What...what did it look like?'

'A crawly, blind thing, all rags and bones.'

'So Jack Thatcher was right, then,' Ned said softly. 'Is that what's taking the stones, d'ye think?'

The hob shrugged. 'I do not know.'

'For a holy place, a lot of bad things happen here,' Ned said.

The hob said nothing.

Ned picked up the lantern and got to his feet. He glanced around uneasily. 'We'd best look in the chapter house before it gets too dark. I don't want to stay here longer than I have to.'

The chapter house had always been the hob's favourite room in the abbey. The brother men had gathered there each morning to talk about abbey matters but when they had finished and gone about their work, it became *his* special place. He still remembered its carved stonework full of tiny, hidden creatures and grotesque faces, and walls painted with strange and wonderful trees and flowers, and holy people and angels. Daylight coming through the coloured glass windows cast small pools of crimson, gold and blue on the tiled floor. He thought of the times he had let the colours dapple his fur as he dozed and dreamed in a patch of warm sunlight. Surely, *surely*, this chamber would still be as he remembered it? Surely something so beautiful would not have been destroyed by the king's men?

The hob followed Ned along the alley, to the passageway leading to the chapter house. The boy stood for a moment by the arched entrance of the passage, the lantern held aloft. It was narrow and high, a cold, dark tunnel of stone and the hob sensed his reluctance to go any further.

The hob went on ahead of the boy to push open the chapter house door and allow the last of the afternoon light to fill the passageway. He stared around in shock at the state of the chamber. The glass in the windows had been smashed and the coloured shards lay scattered across the floor, glimmering like frost in the dusk. The floor tiles had been lifted and taken away, leaving just ghost shapes in the mortar. The stone niches around the monks' seats had been smashed, and all the beasts and strange little faces had been hacked away to lie in rubble and dust on the floor. A feeling of terrible loss squeezed the breath from the hob's body.

Ned climbed onto the stone bench running around the wall. The lantern light picked out a long white wing painted on the wall beside the east window. He lifted the lantern higher and revealed an angel, dressed in a white robe, holding a feather in its hand.

'The nangel,' the hob whispered, old memories stirring in a corner of his mind.

'My mam's sister Bess told me 'bout a dead angel buried in the forest by the monks long ago,' Ned said. 'She always swore it was true, though my mam says it was just a story.'

'Mam's sister was right,' the hob said. 'The nangel was real.'

Ned glanced down at him with a frown. 'How d'ye know?'

'I was living here when its grave was found.'

The boy's eyes widened in astonishment. 'Was it just bones? Did it have wings?'

The hob shook his head. 'I did not see it for myself, but the nangel was not dead.'

Ned climbed down and sat in the abbot's seat. He set the lantern on the bench beside him. His eyes gleamed with excitement. 'Tell me about it.'

The hob sat on a fallen stone and wrapped his tail around his feet to keep them warm. 'One winter, a very long time ago,' he began, 'the Dark King of the Unseelie Court came to the forest, with his band of warrior fays. He caught a hob and cut off his tail. He would have killed him but a nangel appeared and saved the hob's life.'

Ned sat forward, eyes wide. 'Were it *ye*? The hob?'

The hob held up his tail and frowned at Ned. The boy grinned and said, 'Course not. Go on, Brother Walter.'

'The hob escaped when the Dark King turned on the nangel and shot it with an arrow.'

'He *shot* it,' Ned said in a shocked whisper, 'but he didn't kill it?'

'Even a fay king as powerful as him cannot kill a nangel, but the Dark King's magic was strong enough to leave the nangel in a deep sleep for as long as the arrow was in its body. A human from Yagleah found it in the snow and ran to the abbey to tell the brother men. They thought it really *was* dead and they were frightened that their god would be angry, so they buried it in the forest.'

Ned was quiet for several moments. 'So there're fays in the forest?'

'Not so many now, not since...' The hob's voice caught in his throat as dark and painful memories flooded his mind. 'There was a terrible battle between the Seelie and Unseelie fays the summer after the nangel's grave was found. Many of the forest fays died.' The hob gazed into the lantern light, seeing that day again in his mind. A shudder went through him and he looked back up at the boy. 'How did Bess know about the nangel? The brother men kept it secret.'

'She told me her forefather was the man who found the angel and helped the monks to bury it. The story's been told in her family ever since, but we ain't supposed to talk 'bout it to other people, though I think nobody'd believe us if we *did*. Mam always says it ain't true and I ain't sure *I* ever believed it, till now,' Ned said. 'So, who dug it up?'

The hob felt a curious little squeeze of pain in his chest as he remembered another boy, not much older than Ned, and a taciturn fay warrior. 'My friends,' he said softly and with a surge of pride. '*They* took the arrow from the nangel's body and set it free.'

'Where did it go?'

The hob shrugged a shoulder. 'I don't know, but it came back the following spring when a demon attacked the abbey and the villages. It fought the demon and killed it.' He looked up at the angel on the wall. 'I think that is why the brother men painted it here, to remember what it did for them.'

'That ain't something ye're likely to forget,' Ned said, turning to gaze up at the angel.

They sat in silence for a while. A trace of the peace that had always filled this chamber settled over them and the hob was glad; with so much else lost or destroyed, he was glad that something good remained here.

'Why's he holding a feather?' Ned asked.

'The brother men found a feather from its wing in the snow beside it. They kept it locked away in a box for a hundred years. The nangel took it back after it was released from its grave but I think the brother men wanted to remember that they had looked after it for a while.'

'Shame it ain't still here,' Ned said softly, 'though I suppose the king's men would have taken that an' all.' He looked around the chapter house with a frown. The windows framed a sky of twilight blue, scattered with the first few stars and the rising moon. 'I best be getting back to the carts. We'll be starting out for Yagleah soon.' He picked up the lantern and walked to the door where he paused to look back at the hob. 'I left food for ye behind the door in the monks' kitchen, in a box, to keep it safe.'

The hob grinned in delight. 'Thank you!'

Someone out in the cloister called Ned's name.

'I have to go,' Ned said. 'Do ye mind staying here by yerself after dark?'

The hob shook his head. 'Dark is dark. It does not frighten me.'

'What about the evil ghost?'

'I will hide from him.'

'Hide yerself well then,' Ned said. 'I'll see ye tomorrow.' And with that, the boy was gone, taking the light with him.

The hob sat in the middle of the chapter house floor for a while longer, feeling the silence settle around him, deep and still. Countless little white moons were reflected in the shards of broken glass. Above him, the angel was a pale ghost in the gloom. There was a chill in the air and the hob felt the urge to be in his nest, safe and warm. He waited until he was sure the carts had left the abbey, and then ran along the silent cloister alleys, to the kitchen, where he found the box of food on the floor beside the yard door. It was small and not too heavy for him to carry to the barn.

Mist rolling up from the river had turned the yard to a shallow white lake. The western sky glowed with the last of the daylight and a blackbird perched on top of the barn roof sang the sun to its rest.

Keeping a wary eye on the hole in the drain, he crossed the yard. To his relief, he reached the barn and managed to haul the box up the ladder to the hayloft without attracting the boggart's attention.

He settled in his nest and opened the box. By the last of the evening light coming through a gap in the thatch, he saw what the boy had put inside. He barely noticed the bread and cheese, or the apples and dried plums. All he saw were the fat brown hazelnuts. He stroked a shell with a fingertip and could almost taste the nut inside. 'Thank you,' he whispered in delight, 'thank you!'

There was a rustle in the hay and a she-rat was there. He sensed rather than saw her, and felt the small warmth from her body. He shared the cheese and bread with her, and listened to her thoughts. They were full of rat words, but he understood them all the same. She was happy because sharing his food meant she did not have to leave the barn to go scavenging. The night outside held strange things and she wanted no part of them.

What things? the hob asked silently.

The rat stopped eating for a moment. He glimpsed what was in her mind: a creature of bones and trailing rags, shuffling through the shadows. *It comes from the darkest place. Creatures of blood and bone and fur hide from it.*

The crawly man. The hob burrowed a little deeper into the hay. *Is it close by? Is it near the barn?*

Perhaps. It is always watching and waiting.

The hob lay awake long after the she-rat left, listening to the small night noises around the barn, but at last tiredness wrapped soft arms around him and pulled him down into dreams of the forest. He was not sure if the sound of hooves on the cobbles was part of his dream or if a deer had crossed the yard to stand outside the barn door. He was dimly aware that there was something odd about the way the creature moved, as if it walked on two legs, and not four. He stirred restlessly and then settled again, and did not wake until the dawn came in through the gaps in the roof.

Chapter Six

The hob waited in the barn until the carts arrived. He heard voices and the clatter of tools being unloaded. The barn door opened and he crept to the edge of the hayloft to see who was there. He was relieved to see Ned, carrying an armful of branches and kindling. The boy laid the wood beside a makeshift hearth of flat stones and knelt to scrape aside yesterday's ashes. His cheeks and nose were reddened by the cold morning air.

'Thank you for the hazelnuts,' the hob called softly, 'and for the other things too.'

Ned looked relieved to see him. 'I'm right glad ye're safe, Brother Walter, I was worried about ye. Did ye stay here in the barn last night?'

The hob nodded. 'I've made a nest up here in the hayloft.'

Ned wiped his ashy hands on the front of his doublet and got to his feet. 'Did the ghost come lookin' for ye?'

The hob climbed down the ladder. 'No.'

The boy shivered. 'I'll be glad when we don't have to work here no more. Jack Thatcher came to our house last night and said Sir Samuel should come and fetch his own stone, and that it ain't right to disturb whatever's haunting the abbey. Mam said we should listen to Jack and that we don't need Sir Samuel's money, that we'll get by without it.'

'Mam is right,' the hob said. 'And Jack Thatcher too.'

A shiver went through Ned's body and the hob saw apprehension in his dark eyes. He cleared his throat. 'I'm frightened, Brother Walter.'

The hob nodded. 'So am I.'

The hob watched from the doorway as Ned ran across the yard and up the steps to the West Door. He listened for the sound of hammering but it did not come. *Is something wrong?* he wondered. *Shouldn't they have started work by now?* Worried by the silence, he went after Ned. The church was empty and the tools lay on the floor near the scaffolding. The door to the north cloister alley had been propped open with a stone. The hob heard voices and hurried to see what was happening. He peered cautiously around the door jamb and saw Ned and the three men staring up at the roof boss by the church door.

'Well, it *ain't* here now,' Tobias Bodfish said, his thick black brows knitting into a scowl. The hob had a clear view of the boss which yesterday had been the head of the Green Man. Now it was as smooth and round as a river pebble, with not so much as a leaf or a berry to be seen.

'But it *was* there, I swear it,' Ned insisted.

Tobias nodded. 'Ay, I believe ye, boy, but it ain't there *now*, is all I'm sayin'.'

54

Ned hurried along the alley, stopping beneath each boss in turn. 'The others are still here.'

Tobias scratched his bristly chin and muttered, 'They'll probably be gone soon enough, like all the others.' He turned to Noll. 'I tell ye, this place is cursed and no mistake.'

Noll's mouth hardened into a grim line but the hob saw fear in his eyes.

'How are we going to take the other bosses down?' Kit asked.

'I ain't sure,' Noll said. 'I'll ask one of the stonemasons later, when we unload our carts at the manor.'

'Well, if we ain't taking 'em down today, there's nowt to say they'll be here tomorrow,' Tobias said.

Noll turned on him angrily. 'Ye're welcome to try chiselling 'em out of the roof, but I ain't in a hurry to have this lot come down on my head. There has to be a way to do the job safely, and that's what we'll find out from Sir Samuel's stonemasons.' He turned and strode back to the church.

The hob ducked out of sight behind the door jamb. More than likely, Noll would not be able to see him, but he was not taking the risk, just in case.

'Take a look up the stairs, boy,' Tobias said. 'See if there're any stones we've missed.'

Tobias and Kit walked away, leaving Ned to gaze up at the featureless roof boss. The hob went to stand beside him.

'Another one gone,' Ned said. He glanced down at the hob and added hopefully, 'Don't suppose ye want to come with me up the stairs?'

The hob did not want to go, but he could not leave the boy to go alone, so he nodded.

Ned smiled. 'For someone so small, ye have a big and brave spirit, Brother Walter.'

The hob kept close to Ned as they made their way back into the church and along the south aisle to the south transept. In one corner, the night stairs led up to the monks' dorter. They walked up the steep flight of stone steps to a dark little landing. Ned peered cautiously into the long chamber beyond. The sky between the rafters was a pale, cold blue and in the daylight, the hob saw things he had missed when he hid from the boggart two nights ago: several wooden bed frames, hung with cobwebs, pushed together in a corner; the patches of bare stone wall where plaster had fallen away to lie in damp heaps amongst puddles and autumn leaves; broken window shutters. There were no carvings or paintings here.

In the reredorter beyond the dorter, latrines with wooden seats were lined up over the drain far below. Ned peered down through a round hole and wrinkled his nose.

'Phaw! It don't smell too good in here.'

The hob sniffed the air and his fur bristled. 'That is boggart smell. Bad, *bad*.' He pointed to one of the seat holes. 'It lives down there, in the drain.' In his mind, he could see the creature, squatting in the dark, listening to them.

Ned took a hasty step back. 'A *boggart*?'

'They do not like daylight, so we should be safe enough for now.'

'But...a *boggart*?' Ned said. 'They're *real*?'

The hob gave him a hard stare. Humans knew so little about the world they lived in. 'Of course.'

'Could the boggart be the one conjurin' the carvings away?'

The hob snorted at the thought of the creature having that much magic. If it did, it would indeed be dangerous. 'No, and boggarts like treasure, not stones.'

Ned's eyes widened in excitement. 'Maybe it's hiding Abbot Matthew's treasure down there and that's why the king's men didn't find it.'

The hob considered this for a moment. 'It sounds like a boggarty kind of thing to do.'

Ned grinned. 'We'll tell Sir Samuel a boggart's stole his treasure, then. I'd like to see him crawl into the drain to fetch it.'

The hob blew out his cheeks and patted his belly. 'He would get stuck.'

''Cept he'd most likely send *me* to search the drain,' Ned said, pulling a face, 'and the boggart would probably *eat* me.'

They searched the last of the rooms in the east range, finishing in the kitchen, but they were plain and bare.

'Ain't nowhere else to look,' Ned said at last. 'I best get back to the church and tell my father there ain't much else left.'

Ned opened the yard door and looked up at the sky. He rubbed his hands together briskly to warm them. 'Frost tonight, I think.'

The hob sniffed the air and nodded.

'Well, stay warm, Brother Walter, and I'll leave ye some food in the hayloft, in yer box.'

Ned sprinted across the yard, past the well and over to the West Door of the church. He ran up the steps and disappeared inside the building. The hob decided to go and see if any there were any apples left in the orchard, maybe a windfall or two overlooked by the blackbirds.

The hob heard singing coming from the direction of the monks' graveyard. It was Urchin. Deciding the apples could wait for now, he went to look for her.

Wooden boards marked the graves. Each one had a name carved into it. He found one that he remembered from the time he had lived here. The wood was mossy and worn with age, and though the letters had almost weathered away, he knew the shapes had once spelled out the snail brother's name: *Thomas Maslen.* He patted the board, and then sat beside it to watch Urchin, singing as she spun in slow circles between the graves, her arms in the air and her eyes closed. Her voice lilted like birdsong through the autumn air, high and sweet. Her feet did not bend so much as a single stalk of grass.

'Do you know who makes the stones and the paintings on the walls disappear from the abbey?' the hob asked after a while.

Urchin stopped dancing. She put her hands to the sides of her head and spread her fingers. 'The Deerman. He dances 'em all away to the forest.'

The hob remembered the sound of hooves in the yard the previous night and his certainty that whatever it was, it had walked on two feet, not four. A shiver went down his tail as he realised that it had not been part of his dream after all. 'What kind of creature is it?' he asked anxiously.

'Don't know,' Urchin said, shrugging. 'A spirit, mebbe, or a fay.' She started to twirl again, singing as she did so. '*Merry the dance at the old Cold Fair, merry the song and frosty the air.*'

The hob slapped a paw on the ground, keeping time with the song. There had been too little music in his life for far too long.

'*Sing for the King, the beggar, the fool, sing for the winter and welcome in Yule.*'

Her voice trailed away as she slowly faded to a shadow, and then disappeared.

The hob was deep in thought as he made his way to the pigpen and settled in a corner. Who was the Deerman and what did he want with the abbey stones? And what did Urchin mean when she said that

59

the Deerman danced the stones away to the forest? Stones, he was sure, did not dance.

The hob closed his eyes and immediately a grunt and the smell of pig welcomed him. He curled up against the old sow's flank and rubbed her bristly back with his paw.

Have you seen the Deerman?

The pig shifted restlessly. The hob heard her thoughts. She was yearning for something but it was a few moments before he understood what it was. She wanted to leave the abbey with the Deerman.

But who is the Deerman? What is he? If he's a creature of the forest, why have I never come across him before?

The pig did not know. All she knew for certain was that she wanted to follow him back to the forest. Only, she wasn't sure how to do that.

The hob patted her shoulder. *Don't worry, I will help you if I can.*

Mary Magdalene grunted again, a contented noise deep in her throat, and settled down to sleep.

Tonight, the hob decided, *I will watch out for the Deerman. I will see what he does with the stones and the painted people from the walls.* He stretched his arms above his head and yawned widely. *But now, it is time for a nap.*

Chapter Seven

That night, long after Ned and the men had gone home to Yagleah, the hob hid in the reeds beside the abbey bridge. He had a clear view of the causeway across the flood meadows, leading from the track to the abbey gate. If anything came out of the forest that night, he would see it.

Around him, the frosted world glimmered white in the moonlight and in spite of his thick winter fur, he shivered in the icy chill.

'So cold! So, *so* cold!' he murmured through chattering teeth. He thought longingly of his nest in the barn and the food Ned had shared with him today and hoped the Deerman would be here soon.

The stars slowly crossed the sky and the hob's eyes grew heavy. Even the bitter cold could not stop him from dozing. When he woke the moon was tangled in the branches of the alder trees beside the causeway. Ice crusted his fur and numbed his paws, but his discomfort was forgotten when he saw a glowing wisp of green mist on the bridge. It quickly began to fade. Something had passed this way, just moments before, heading to the abbey. The hob struggled to his feet and hurried to the gatehouse, anxious to follow the mist before it disappeared altogether. The gate stood open and the trail of greenish light shone faintly on the yard cobbles. It led to the West Door of the church.

As the hob crossed the yard, the boggart crawled out of the hole in the drain and squatted beside it. Moonlight silvered the thick dark fur on its back and glinted in its eyes. The hob gasped in fright as it broke into a lurching lope, heading straight for him.

The hob turned and fled back under the gateway arch, across the bridge and along the causeway. He slowed down when he reached the edge of the forest. Where should he hide? Instinct took over and he decided the best way was up, into the branches of an ash tree.

He climbed quickly, his heartbeat pounding in his ears as he scrambled from branch to branch, until he was half way up the tree. He saw the boggart in the distance, sitting on the bridge, its heavy shoulders hunched forward and its head casting from side to side as it sniffed the air to catch his scent.

'Ha!' the hob muttered angrily, his fur still bristling from fright. 'Nasty old boggart.'

The boggart turned and loped slowly back to the gatehouse, where it disappeared into the darkness.

The hob was not in any hurry to leave the safety of the tree. For all he knew, the boggart was lying in wait for him by the gate, and there was no other way in. The high stone walls surrounding the abbey kept things out and kept things in. He had no choice but to stay where he was until dawn, so he settled himself as comfortably as he could in the crook between a branch and the trunk. The tree's spirit stirred in its sleep and he was glad of its reassuring presence.

The hob wiled away the time gazing at the stars and humming softly to himself, until his attention was caught by a faint but growing light in the yard beyond the gatehouse. Something was leaving the abbey, and coming this way. Was it the Deerman? The hob sat up straight, his song forgotten and his heart beating a little faster.

The Deerman was so tall he had to bow his head to pass under the gatehouse arch. A soft greenish glow flickered like marsh lights around his thin body and left a trail on the ground behind him. He was the strangest creature the hob had ever seen, partly an animal, partly a man. He had the head of a deer, with wide, branching antlers, but stood upright like a man and had long-fingered hands, as thin and white as bone. Beneath the hem of a cloak of wispy green rags, the hob could see hooves. The Deerman held a wooden staff, wrapped around with ivy and holly, and above his antlers, things circled and glinted gold and silver in the moonlight. At first the hob thought they were birds, but as they came closer, he was astonished to see that they were fish, swimming in the frosty air.

The Deerman crossed the bridge and walked along the causeway. He reached the ash tree and lifted his head to gaze up through the branches at the hob. The hob looked down into the creature's dark eyes and felt an odd stirring of recognition. He had never seen the Deerman before – he had never even *heard* of him – but deep inside, he knew him; he felt he had always known him. For all the Deerman's strange appearance, a sense of peace surrounded him. As he crouched there, the hob understood the old pig's longing to follow the Deerman into the forest; he was filled with the same strong desire.

The fish wove between the Deerman's antlers. Their scales gleamed like tiny polished coins and the moon was reflected in their black eyes. The creature lowered his head and walked on into the forest. The green glow faded into the shadows between the trees.

The hob did not move for a long time. His thoughts were full of the Deerman and he yearned to see him again, a feeling so strong it was almost painful.

At last, forcing his frozen limbs to move, the hob climbed down from the tree and set off back to the abbey. He hoped the boggart had gone back to its drain but even so, he paused by the main gate to watch and listen for any hint that the boggart was hiding nearby, waiting to pounce. He reached the yard and peered cautiously around the corner of the gatehouse but there was no sign of the creature.

'Go to him, Brother Walter, he needs yer help,' someone whispered close to his ear. He turned quickly, recognising Urchin's voice, but he could not see her. The soft voice came again, more urgently this time, 'Ye must hurry, 'afore the crawlin' man comes...'

'Who needs me?' the hob asked anxiously. 'Where?'

'T'monks' garden...' she said, sounding faint and far off.

'*Who* needs me?' he asked again but there was no reply.

64

For a while he stood and shivered beneath the gatehouse arch, not sure what to do. The thought of going into the cloister terrified him; what if the crawling man was there, creeping through the darkness?

But somebody needed his help and he could not turn away from them, whoever they were. *Perhaps if I run very fast, the crawly thing will not be able to catch me.* Taking a deep breath, the hob scurried across the yard and into the kitchen.

The cloister door stood open. It would soon be dawn and the first faint grey light softened the shadows. The hob peered cautiously along the alleys and through the arches to the frosty garden. There was no sign of the crawling man, but *something* was here. He could hear soft, agitated whimpering, coming from a pile of dead leaves at the far end of the west alley. He edged towards it, stopping only to arm himself with a stout length of broken branch.

'It left me all alone by myself,' something whispered, sounding close to tears. 'Gone and made me all warm and breathey and soft.'

The hob prodded the leaf pile with his branch. 'Come out!' he said gruffly, hoping he sounded more fierce than he felt.

The whispering stopped instantly. The hob waited, and then rustled the pile again. 'Show yourself.'

The pile shifted and a head poked up through the leaves. The hob stared into a pair of large eyes, honey gold and wide with fear. He glanced up and saw the smooth surface of two roof bosses overhead and realised what must have happened: the Deerman had brought the stone hob and the fish to life. It had taken the fish to the forest with it, but why had it left the hob behind?

'Come out here where I can see you properly,' the hob said.

The creature crawled out from beneath the leaves and slowly got to its feet. It was a skinny scrap of a thing, with silken grey fur and a dark tuft on the end of its tail. It held something in a shaking paw and the hob caught a gleam of gold between its fingers. The little hob cleared its throat. 'You are what I see when there are puddles on the floor. Are you one of me?'

The hob nodded. 'We are hobs.'

'Hobs,' the creature said in wonder. 'Nobody told me I was *hobs* before.'

'Do you have a name?'

'Yes! Yes!' The small hob nodded vigorously. 'Curious.'

'Curious?' the hob asked. '*That* is your name?' It was an odd thing to be called.

Curious nodded again. 'And *hobs*.'

'I am Brother Walter.'

The hob caught a movement out of the corner of his eye. Urchin, little more than a wisp of blue mist in the gathering light, drifted through the garden amongst the weeds and brambles.

'*Ye must go!*' Her voice was an urgent whisper in the stillness of the cloister.

The hob looked around in fright. There was nothing to see, but there was a change in the atmosphere, a strange prickle in the air that made his fur bristle uncomfortably. He grabbed Curious's arm. 'Follow me!'

Hauling the terrified creature behind him, the hob ran back to the kitchen. Curious staggered and slipped along, clearly not used to having legs that moved or large hairy feet, but the hob did not dare slow down. When they reached the yard door, Curious gave a yelp and clung to the doorpost.

'*Nonono!*'

'What's the matter?' the hob asked in alarm.

Curious peered up at the sky fearfully. The pink glow of a frosty dawn rose in the east but overhead, the sky was still dark. 'The big blackness ...the world has gone away.' He turned and set off back across the kitchen, heading for the cloister, but the hob caught his arm and hung on.

'*No*! We have to leave *now*! The crawly man is coming.' He pulled the whimpering and cowering little creature back to the doorway and out into the yard. Curious put an arm over his head and closed his eyes, but he did not resist as the hob led him towards the barn. The icy cobbles proved a sore trial and every few steps he slipped and fell. The hob watched the kitchen doorway anxiously as he helped Curious to his feet each time and he gave a heartfelt sigh of relief when they reached the barn.

'I think we're safe now,' the hob said as he pushed Curious ahead of him up the ladder to the hayloft. By the light coming through the gaps in the thatch, he could see the small hob crouching there, shaking and whimpering.

'It's gone!' Curious whispered in anguish. 'The gleamy thing. I dropped it and it's gone.'

'We'll look for it later.'

The hob squatted by the edge of the loft and peered down at the barn door. Nothing had come after them, it seemed. He breathed out in relief, and felt his body relax. He was just about to turn away when the barn door slowly creaked open.

Chapter Eight

The hob watched as a shaft of dawn light sliced across the earthen floor far below him. To his horror, a bony hand with blackened nails felt its way through the gap and the crawling man shuffled into the barn. It knelt there, listening, malevolence oozing from it. The hob felt panic rise up to choke him. Behind him, he heard Curious chitter in terror. The thing on the barn floor heard it too; the dreadful head lifted and the withered lips drew back in a snarl that turned the hob's heart to ice. It crawled towards the loft ladder, but the hob darted forward and pushed the ladder as hard as he could. It slid sideways and fell to the floor with a crash, sending up clouds of dust and hay. The crawling man did not slow or even flinch. It reached one of the timber posts supporting the loft and, digging its nails into the wood, slowly began to climb. The hob stared in horror; it would not take long for the creature to reach the loft, and then what?

The hob glanced up at the holes in the roof. If they could just reach one, they could get out of the barn. He looked around and saw a pile of old wicker baskets in a corner.

'Quickly,' he said, hauling Curious to his feet. 'The crawly man is coming. We have to escape. Help me pile up the baskets.'

Curious looked confused. 'What is baskets?'

'These are,' the hob said, grabbing one from the pile and dragging it over to the patch of light beneath the largest hole.

Curious hurried to fetch another one.

The stack of baskets quickly grew. It swayed alarmingly as the hob began to climb, but it held and he reached the rafters. His heart leaped in terror as he saw the top of the crawling man's head draw level with the loft floor. Wisps of grey hair barely covered its peeling scalp.

'Hurry, Curious!' the hob urged.

A hand appeared over the edge of the loft, and dug its nails into the gap between two floorboards. The creature began to haul itself up. Curious threw himself at the baskets. They creaked and tilted as he scrambled up and the hob thought it would collapse before Curious could reach the rafters. Just as the baskets began to slip sideways, Curious made a wild leap for safety, and the hob managed to grab his tail. For a moment, the small hob dangled in the air, limbs flailing. Bracing his feet on the rafters, the hob hauled him up. Curious scrabbled desperately for the beam and clung on, whimpering with fear. By now, the creature was crawling across the loft, its face turned towards the sound of the hobs high above it. The baskets lay scattered across the floor and the hob felt a surge of relief; the crawling man would not be able to reach them now.

But then the thing shuffled its way over to the barn wall. The hob watched in dismay as it found finger holds between the timbers and began to climb again.

'Oh *no!*' the hob breathed. He pointed to the hole in the roof. 'We have to get up there *now*.'

With much scrabbling, the hob reached up and got a grip on the icy thatch. He pulled himself up through the gap and onto the roof, then reached down and grabbed Curious's paws to help him up. The hob could not see the crawling man, but he could hear it and it sounded frighteningly close.

'This way,' the hob said. He slid down the slope of the thatched roof towards the branches of an elder tree growing behind the barn. Curious was close behind him and they climbed down through the tree and into the small strip of pasture between the barn and the river. Only then did the hob feel a measure of safety. But where could they hide? Where would they be safe?

In the morning light, the frosty fields and woods were ghostly pale and glittering. The reed beds along the river margins bristled with ice and the trees in the forest were misty clouds against the pink dawn sky. A couple of stars still shone faintly and the moon hung between them, as fragile as a white petal.

Curious gazed around, his eyes wide and his mouth open. The hob knew this must all seem so extraordinary to him. There was so much for him to discover but it would have to wait for now. They were not safe from the crawly thing yet.

The hob stared across the river at the forest. They could hide there until the carts came from Yagleah. He led Curious down the riverbank to the bridge and along the causeway to the forest. He found a hollow beneath the roots of a fallen tree. From here they had a good view of the causeway. He could not see the crawly man.

Now that the immediate danger had passed, weariness settled over the hob and he tried to make himself as comfortable as he could. It was only the thought of leaving Urchin and the old pig behind that stopped him from taking Curious deep into the forest. If there was any way at all that he could help the pig to leave the abbey with the Deerman, and find Urchin's father, then he had to do it. *Hobs do not run away when their friends need them*, he thought, *not ever*.

Looking at Curious, he was disturbed to see him shivering violently and was dismayed to realise that the little hob did not have a winter coat. Without a good undergrowth of thick winter fur, he could easily die from the cold.

'We will find something warm to wrap you in as soon as we get back to the abbey,' the hob said.

Curious nodded and his breath clouded around his head. There was a faraway look in his eyes, as if he had stopped trying to understand this strange world he found himself in.

The hob watched the track, willing Ned and the others to hurry. He wrapped his tail around Curious and rubbed the hob's arms to try to keep him warm.

'I w-would like to go b-back to my p-p-place in the r-r-roof now,' Curious whispered, his teeth chattering. 'P-p-please?'

'I don't know how to make that happen,' the hob said. 'But things will not seem so bad, once you get used to being alive.'

Curious drew himself into a small, unhappy huddle and closed his eyes tightly. 'Make it all go away,' he whispered.

The hob said nothing. What could he say? There was nothing they could do now but wait.

***

Far off along the track, the carts swayed into view. The hob waited until they passed by before pulling Curious to his feet and setting off after them. Ned, sitting on the seat board of the second cart, glanced over his shoulder. His smile when he saw the hob gave way to an open-mouthed stare when he saw Curious. He said something to his father, then jumped down from the cart and ran back to where the hob and Curious were hiding, while the carts continued on their way.

'*Another* hob!' Ned stared at the miserable and shivering Curious in amazement. 'Where'd ye find this 'un?'

'He came from the stone in the roof near the brother men's garden,' the hob said. 'His name is Curious.'

Without a word, Ned took off his brown woollen scarf and held it out to Curious, who stared at it blankly. The hob took the scarf and wrapped it around Curious's body. He could not move his arms but it would keep him warm for now.

'Thank you,' the hob said.

Ned shrugged awkwardly. 'I'll bring something better for him to wear tomorrow. Can he talk?'

'Yes,' Curious said, his voice muffled behind the scarf.

'So... ye really are *alive*?'

Curious nodded. He worked his paws free from beneath the scarf and squatted on the track, shoulders hunched and unhappiness clouding his golden eyes.

Ned pulled a face. 'Well, it doesn't seem to please ye much.' He turned to the hob. 'Do ye know who magicked him out of the stone?'

'The Deerman,' the hob said.

'Who?'

The hob wondered how to explain the Deerman to the boy when he did not fully understand it himself. 'He is a creature from the forest, neither mortal nor fay. He has antlers and hooves and the ghost girl calls him the Deerman.'

Ned looked startled. 'The *ghost* girl?'

The hob sighed. There was so much to *explain*. 'She died at the abbey. I do not know when, but she has been waiting ever since for her father to come back for her.'

Ned nodded slowly as he took this in. 'Oh.'

'She's...shy. And very nice. She saved me from the boggart *and* the crawly man.' The hob patted Curious on the head. 'She saved us both.'

74

Ned cleared his throat nervously. 'Did she save ye from the Deerman an' all?'

'The Deerman would never harm us,' the hob said. He was sure of that without knowing why. He saw the boy shiver and felt sorry for him. Humans were always shocked to discover they were living so close to creatures they told stories about but never believed in, whether they were ghosts or fays or things from the darkest places of old magic.

'Why's he taking the creatures out of the stones,' Ned asked with a quaver in his voice, 'this Deerman?'

The hob gazed sadly towards the abbey. 'To save them.'

'From what?'

The hob turned to look up at the boy. 'From you. Humans. You will smash them all into pieces, sooner or later, and then they will be lost and gone forever.'

'So why'd he leave *him* behind?' Ned nodded towards Curious.

Before the hob could reply, Curious said, 'I wanted to go with him but he told me to stay. He took the shiny things away, but not *me.*'

'The fish,' the hob explained, seeing Ned's questioning look.

'The ones from the roof boss?' Ned asked. 'They're gone an' all?'

The hob nodded.

75

'What ye doing out here in the cold?'

'We are escaping from the crawly man.'

Ned's frost-nipped face sharpened with worry. 'He came after ye *again*? That's bad. I'm right glad he didn't catch ye, though.' He glanced over his shoulder at the carts, already far in the distance. 'I best catch up with the others, 'fore they come looking for me. Told 'em I needed to wee. I'll leave some food for ye both in the barn, up in the hayloft.'

By the time the hob and Curious reached the abbey yard, Ned and the men were at work in the church. The hob led Curious back to the barn. He was tired to his bones and wanted nothing more than to burrow into his nest and sleep the day away.

Curious gave an excited squeak and picked up something from amongst the wisps of hay on the floor. He held it out to the hob. 'My gleamy thing!'

It was a golden acorn. It might have been stone once, like the small hob, but it was made of gold now, light and thin and each detail beautifully carved to make the acorn look realistic. The hob took it and felt a tingle in his fingers. There was magic here, he realised, strong and old and much, much bigger than the acorn that held it. But whose magic was it? Not the man who had carved the stone hob, he was sure. All the Crowfield Abbey stones were carved by humans and humans did not have this kind of magic inside them, even if sometimes they thought they did.

76

Perhaps it was the Deerman's magic, the hob thought. Somewhere inside him, fear tangled together with awe and longing in a confusing bundle. All he knew as he gazed down at the acorn was that he wanted to see the Deerman again; more than that, he wanted to follow him back into the forest, just as the fish and all the other carved stones and wall paintings had done.

There were so many puzzling things in the abbey, with answers hidden and hard to find. He would just have to wait and be patient, and let them unfold in their own time.

The hob handed the acorn to Curious. 'Keep it very safe,' he said.

Curious nodded and clutched it to his chest.

Someone had retrieved the ladder and leaned it against the edge of the hayloft. The hobs climbed it wearily. To the hob's delight, he found bread, hazelnuts and apples inside the box in the hayloft. Ned had been as good as his word.

The hob divided his nest of hay in two to make a bed for Curious.

Curious took a hazelnut from the box and sniffed it. 'Is this a stone?'

The hob took it from him and cracked it between his teeth. He prised the soft nut from the shell and held it out. 'Taste it.'

Curious nibbled the nut, and then nodded. 'I like this.' He picked up the discarded shell and crunched it for a moment, then spat the pieces out into his paw. 'I do *not* like the bones.'

'That is the shell,' the hob said, 'and you don't eat it. Just the nut inside.'

Curious picked up the bread. 'Is this a nut too?'

'Bread,' the hob said sleepily. He settled himself in his nest and ate an apple. His chilled body gradually warmed up as his stomach filled.

'Brother Walter?'

'Hmmm?'

'Where did the crawly thing go?'

'I don't know,' the hob said, 'but I do not think we have seen the last of it.'

The hob yawned and closed his eyes. Sleep was there, waiting for him, ready to stir dreams though his mind.

After what only seemed like moments, the hob woke to the sound of people talking in the barn below the loft. He was surprised to realise that the whole morning had passed and Ned and the men had stopped work to eat their midday meal. Curious, buried under a pile of hay, snored in soft little wheezes. The hob did not disturb him. A sleeping Curious was less likely to attract attention than a wakeful one.

The hob crept to the edge of the loft and peered over. A fire burned on the hearth and the smoke threaded up through the holes in the roof. He saw Ned's gaze flicker upwards and for a moment, their eyes met. Ned nodded and winked but his mouth trembled and his face was pale beneath the streaks of dirt. The hob had the feeling that something had frightened him very badly.

'Ain't no use pretending I didn't see what I seen,' Tobias said stubbornly. He glared at Noll. 'It was a girl and I saw right through her, like she were just made o' fog.'

Kit frowned at Tobias from beneath the brim of his woollen cap. His thin face was chalk white beneath the freckles. 'What would a *girl* be doin' in an abbey, ghost or otherwise?'

'I don't know, but I saw her looking around one of the pillars in the nave.'

'That's enough,' Noll said. 'Yer mind's playing tricks on ye.' But the hob could see he did not really believe this. His eyes gave him away and he looked anywhere but at Tobias's face. He picked at his teeth with a sharp bit of straw and spat something out onto the floor.

'She was there,' Tobias growled. 'Jack Thatcher seen summat bad, and now I seen *her*. This ain't a good place to be, Noll.'

'Jack Thatcher ain't coming back,' Noll said evenly, 'and if the rest of us take it into our heads this place is haunted, we ain't never going to finish our work, and we won't be paid.'

79

'Not that 'is lordship's payin' a fair wage,' Tobias muttered angrily, 'because he ain't. He steals our common land for his sheep, pulls down our houses, and then pays us half of what we're worth for an honest day's work. It was a bad day when *he* came to live at t'manor. He ain't like his father at all. Old Sir Giles were always a fair man and he looked after us, right and proper. The steward, Dunch, seems decent enough, but he does what Sir Samuel tells him.' He lifted his jug to his mouth and took a swig of beer and scowled into the flames. With his black hair and beard and heavy dark brows, the hob thought Tobias looked very like the boggart. Even his forearms and fingers bristled with black hair. *And he does not smell a great deal better than the boggart, either.*

Ned and the men finished their meal in silence, then started to gather up their baskets and jugs.

'Say what ye like, '*tis* haunted,' Tobias said at last, getting to his feet, 'an' we all know it. What about that...that *thing* Jack Thatcher saw? That weren't no trick o' the mind.'

'I said, *enough!*' There was a hard edge to Noll's voice. 'Back to work, all o' ye.'

Noll left the barn. Kit stood in a corner to relieve himself, and then hurried after him. Ned hung back while Tobias doused the fire with the dregs from his beer jug. Malty-smelling steam hissed up in a small cloud.

Tobias wrapped his grubby brown scarf around his neck. He leaned towards Ned and lowered his voice. 'Jack said the thing he saw were *evil*. Said it turned its face to him and its eyes were milky-like, but he were sure the thing could *hear* where he was. Said there were a look of malice on its withered old face that were chillin' to see. Ye keep yer wits about ye, young Ned. An' if ye see owt, yell.'

Tobias pulled the brim of his old woollen hat over his ears and left the barn. Ned waited until he was gone, then looked up at the hob. 'Did ye hear all that?'

The hob nodded.

'Ye can come home with us, if ye like. Our house is full to the rafters with people and babies, and dogs and the like, but ye can't stay here.'

The hob stared at Ned in delight. Home! The boy was offering them a *home*! It would be somewhere warm to spend the winter months.

And then he remembered Urchin and the pig and he shook his head regretfully.

'I cannot leave the girl alone with the crawly thing,' the hob said. 'I have to find her father, so she can leave the abbey with him. *Then* we'll come home with you.'

Ned raised an eyebrow. 'And how d'ye mean to do that?'

'He's waiting for her at the Cold Fair. I will look for him there, just as soon as I find out where it is.'

Ned snorted. 'I wish ye luck with that! Ain't been a Cold Fair in Yagleah since my father's grandfather was a boy. Last one brought the sweatin' sickness to the village and farms all round, and lots of people died. After that, the fair was moved to Lammas. The girl's father must have died *long* since.'

The hob stared at him in dismay. How would he find Urchin's father now?

'Though...' Ned paused for a moment, 'I've heard tales of people seeing a ghostly fair up on Yagleah common around St Francis' day, when the old fair used to start. Jack Thatcher swears he saw it when he was a boy.'

'A ghost fair?' The hob was not sure he liked the sound of that.

Ned shrugged. 'So people say. Maybe the girl's father is a ghost an' all, and is still at the fair.'

'Ned! Come on, boy, we ain't got all day!' Tobias called from the yard.

Ned pulled a face and hurried to the barn door. 'If ye change yer mind about coming home with us, hide on our cart at dusk. Ye can always come back here with us on the cart in the morning. The ghost girl will likely be safe enough for now, if she's managed to escape from the crawling man this long.'

The hob returned to his nest in a thoughtful mood. Ned was right; Urchin had kept out of the crawly man's way so far, and he could always come back tomorrow and see her, so she did not have to be alone. And then, if the ghost of the Cold Fair really did haunt Yagleah common, and if Urchin's father was still there, then there might be a chance of bringing father and daughter together again. The hob settled deep in the hay. The thought of the ghostly fair filled him with dread but if he did not go and search for Urchin's father, then nobody else would. The simple truth was that he was the ghost girl's only hope of ever seeing her father again.

Chapter Nine

The hob went to search for Urchin that afternoon, to ask what her father looked like. The graveyard was a good place to start, he decided. She seemed to like being there. Curious trailed along behind him, shivering with cold in spite of being wrapped in Ned's scarf. It had taken a lot of persuasion to make him leave his acorn behind in the loft for safekeeping and even as they crossed the yard, Curious glanced back towards the barn, a forlorn expression on his face.

'Your acorn will still be there when we get back,' the hob assured him.

'My paw feels too empty,' Curious said.

'Paws are meant to be empty,' the hob said, 'mostly. That way, they're all ready when you need to put something in them.'

'Oh,' Curious said, but he did not look any happier. He stopped beside a pile of horse dung and leaned down to sniff it. He straightened up hurriedly and sneezed, then poked his fingers into his nostrils. He stared around with a wild look in his eyes.

'What's the matter?' the hob asked.

'The nose colours,' Curious said. 'They are not *nice*.'

The hob pulled Curious's hands away from his nose. 'They are smells.'

'Smells?' Curious said doubtfully.

'Everything has a smell, like a shadow that *you* can't see but your nose can.'

Curious took another cautious sniff, while eyeing the dung warily. 'The shadow from this is very bad. What is it?'

The hob opened his mouth to reply, and then closed it again. Explaining horse dung to Curious was going to take some time. It would have to wait. 'I will tell you later.'

The hob steered wide of the hole in the drain. When they reached the pigpen, he pointed to the shelter behind the brambles. 'Wait for me there. Sit in the corner, close your eyes and the old pig will be there to keep you warm.'

Curious peered over the tangle of brambles, a worried look puckering his face. 'What is *old pig*? Is it like a fire?'

The hob shook his head. It was easy to forget that Curious knew very little about the world beyond his upside down corner of the cloister. 'She is an animal, and she is my friend. But you must keep your eyes closed or you will not find her.'

Curious looked bemused but he just nodded. He knelt down and edged his way through the brambles. The scarf snagged on thorns, untangling bits of wool, but with a lot of sighing and muttering, he finally reached the shelter at the back of the pen and settled himself in a corner.

The hob saw Curious close his eyes. A look of surprise crossed the small hob's face. It quickly turned to delight as he settled against

85

the invisible pig. The hob heard snuffly grunts and smelled the familiar pig smell and nodded, satisfied that Curious was safe enough for now.

The hob heard Urchin before he saw her. He followed the sound of singing through the garden and between the graves. He did not see her at first, hidden as she was behind an ancient yew tree, but he found her sitting on the frosty grass in the lee of the graveyard wall.

Urchin smiled at him. 'I seen the Deerman bring the fay and the fishes out o' the stones, but he told t'little fay to stay behind. I were worried that the crawlin' man would catch him, but I'm glad ye found him first.'

The hob grimaced. 'It *nearly* caught us both but we hid in the forest.'

She lifted her face to the early morning sunlight. 'Ent nobody safe from the crawlin' man for long. Ye take care, liddle Walter.'

The hob nodded. He sat back on his heels and held his tail clear of the frozen ground. 'I liked your song yesterday.'

Urchin looked pleased. 'I sang it at t'fair. People stopped to listen and throw coins. Pappy's a chapman, but he plays a bagpipe too, and I sing with him.' Her smile faded and she got to her feet. The light shone through her as if she was made of painted glass. ''Tis almost time for the Cold Fair. Can feel it tugging me bones, but I can't go there. What if Pappy's waitin' for me?'

The hob wondered whether or not he should tell her that her father and all the people she had known at the fair were long since dead, but he decided not to, in case she lost hope. 'If you tell me what he looks like, I will go and look for him, and bring him here.'

'Ye'll really do that for me?' she asked, her eyes shining with tears. She wiped them away with the back of her hand. ''S name's Jack Gaudy, and he wears a coat o' patches, all blue 'n' red 'n' green. He sells fairings. He has pins an' braid, an' ribbons of silk 'n' satin, an' pretty tin brooches. Please, tell him to *hurry*,' she finished, her voice quivering with longing. The tears spilled down her cheeks. Before the hob could promise her he would do his best, she had vanished.

The hob set off back to the pigpen, humming Urchin's song as he walked along the path beside the orchard. *It should be easy to find Jack Gaudy*, he thought, *with his coat of coloured patches and his bagpipe, though I don't know what a bagpipe is, but Ned might. He will tell me what to look for.*

The late afternoon sun unrolled long shadows behind the apple trees and briefly burnished the last few leaves to copper and gold. A robin sang from the top of a fence post, a little touch of scarlet amongst the faded autumn colours.

The hob gasped as he walked into a rank-smelling cloud. The foul stink turned his stomach and left him struggling for breath. He realised a moment too late where the stench was coming from.

No more than five paces away, the boggart squatted in the middle of the path, watching him.

Chapter Ten

The Boggart's small crimson eyes blinked and squinted in the fading daylight. It waved a viciously clawed hand in the direction of the pigpen and jabbered in agitation.

Two things occurred to the hob in quick succession: the boggart was trying to tell him something important, and more surprisingly, the creature did not seem to be in a hurry to harm him.

The hob cleared his throat. In a shaking voice he said, 'I don't know what you are saying.'

The boggart jabbed a finger towards the pigpen again, and then towards the yard, and grunted.

Had something happened to Curious? Was *that* what the boggart was telling him? The creature got to its feet and loped away along the path to the yard.

I hope this is not some boggarty trick and that it means to eat me, the hob thought anxiously. *Maybe it has already eaten Curious, though it would have to have eaten him very quickly, because I haven't been gone for long.*

The boggart reached the garden gate and paused. It peered back to see if the hob was following, then set off again, its powerful shoulders hunched as it took its weight on its knuckly fists.

The hob ran after it and found it squatting by the empty pigpen. He looked around and called, 'Curious! Where are you?'

But there was only silence. Curious had gone.

The boggart lifted one hand and slowly wiggled its fingers, making them crawl though the air, and pointed to the yard.

Was the creature saying that the crawly man had taken Curious? *Or does it want me to think that, so it can lead me into a trap? Why capture one hob when you can have two?* The hob stared at the boggart warily, fearing to trust him.

The boggart set off again and after a moment's hesitation, the hob followed. When he reached the yard gate, he peered around the edge cautiously. The boggart was squatting by the drain. It saw him and pointed to the hole in the paving stones.

'Oh *no!*' the hob breathed in horror. Curious must be down in the boggart's lair, and the creature wanted him to go down there too. Before he could decide what to do, he saw a movement over by the gatehouse. There, on its hands and knees and creeping stealthily out from the gloom beneath the archway, was the crawling man, its blind eyes white and unblinking as it sniffed the air. Its head jerked around and the hob realised it had caught the boggart's scent. *Though it would be difficult not to,* he thought in disgust.

The crawling man moved with frightening speed towards them, bones scraping on cobbles, rags and skin trailing behind it. Without stopping to think, the hob ran to the drain and jumped down into the hole. The boggart was close behind him, grunting and snuffling. It smelled even worse in the enclosed space and the hob put

90

his paws across his nose and mouth. The boggart prodded him in the back with a claw and, desperately hoping he had not just made a terrible mistake, the hob stumbled off into the gloom.

The drain was a tunnel of stone, high enough for the hob to stand upright. A white light wavered up ahead and the hob could make out an arched roof and walls, streaked with lime. A stream flowed ankle deep along the sloping bottom of the drain, heading down to the river. The water had worn a channel in the mud. The hob tried to climb up onto the narrow ledge against the wall, but his feet slipped on the wet mud and every few steps, he splashed back down into the water. The boggart kept nudging and poking him, urging him to hurry. He glanced back to see if the crawling man was following them, but the boggart's body blocked his view.

The hob stumbled over something in the water. He paused just long enough to see a human skull and a scatter of bones beneath the surface of the clear stream, eerily pale in the white light.

'*Fnurf*,' the boggart huffed, knuckling him in the back. The hob hurried on.

An iron lantern hung from a branch wedged into a crack in the drain wall. By its light, the hob saw a pile of stone blocks lying in the stream. Closer to, he saw that the boggart had broken a hole through the wall and had tunnelled into the earth. The tunnel sloped away downhill and a second white light shone at the far end. This, he was sure, was the creature's lair.

The boggart gabbled something and pointed to the tunnel. The hob hesitated. *If I go in there, I will be trapped.* He heard the crawling man splashing along the stream towards them and thought in desperation, *I have no choice; I have to trust the boggart.* He clambered into the tunnel and ran towards the light.

Wooden planks made an uneven but dry walkway to the boggart's lair. More planks held up the roof and kept the walls from collapsing inwards. Twigs, stones and small pieces of glass dangled from the timbers overhead and the hob ducked to avoid them. A low wall of square stones stood across the entrance to the lair, probably to keep out the water if the drain and tunnel flooded. The hob climbed over and stared around in astonishment.

The boggart's possessions were piled against the plank-lined walls. The floor was paved with floor tiles taken from the abbey. Rusty iron lanterns hung from brackets nailed to the walls. A white flame flickered in each one and the hob held out a paw to the lantern beside the entrance. The flame did not give off any heat and he realised that somehow, the boggart was using fay fire to light his lair. *The creature would need strong magic to do such a thing,* the hob thought uneasily. Fay fire could be dangerous; it led the unwary astray in marshes and on lonely roads, and it danced above the graves of the dead. He had never heard of anyone *catching* the small cold flames before, and trapping them inside lanterns. The idea that a boggart, of all creatures, could do such a thing was hard to believe. Had someone given the fay fire to him?

'Brother Walter!' Curious appeared from behind a wooden chest, grinning with delight. 'The smelly thing saved you too!'

Relief surged through the hob. 'It did not try to harm you, did it?'

Curious shook his head. 'Though my feet are cold and covered in wet ground.' He held up a foot; his fur was caked with mud. 'And he wants my warm scoff.'

'Scarf,' the hob corrected him. He looked uncertainly at the boggart, who was squatting at the far end of the tunnel, peering back along the drain.

'We are safe here. He told me these will protect us from the crawly thing.' Curious pointed to the odd assortment of objects hanging from the roof: magpie feathers and holey stones, small bronze bells, sprigs of mistletoe and rowan, all dangling from lengths of red and blue woollen yarn, tied to twigs pushed between the planks. There was a puzzled look in Curious's eyes. 'But *how* will they do that?'

'Magic,' the hob said. Which by now he suspected the boggart knew how to use very well indeed.

Curious watched a bell slowly twirl on the end of a piece of blue yarn. He reached up and tapped it. It gave a soft *dink*. '*That* will make the crawly man go away?' he asked doubtfully.

93

The hob waved a paw towards the tunnel and all the small hanging things gently swaying in the cold draught. 'All of them together will keep him away.' He hoped that was true, and that the boggart's magic was indeed strong.

'The monks had bells,' Curious said slowly, 'but *they* didn't always keep evil things away.'

The hob said nothing but he remembered only too well the demon that had escaped from beneath the church floor, and how it had brought the huge bells in the tower crashing down. Those bells had not stopped the demon, and they were so much bigger than the boggart's little bronze bells.

The boggart loped along the tunnel and sat down at the entrance to its lair. Pale little lamp flames were reflected in its red eyes. Its black fur was, the hob thought, surprisingly clean for something that lived in a drain, but its rank smell filled the chamber. It said something but the guttural jumble of words meant nothing to the hob. To his astonishment, Curious understood.

'We must not touch his treasure,' Curious said.

The hob glanced around the lair. He saw wicker baskets stacked with cracked and chipped pots and bowls, a pile of broken window glass glinting with fay light and a heap of cloths, stained and mildewed. There were broken knives and dented candlesticks, and charred pages from the monks' books pinned to the earth walls with twigs and thorns. What he did *not* see was treasure.

'I will try not to,' the hob said, wrinkling his nose at the smell coming from a dead crow, hanging by its feet from a braid of red wool. Its blue-black wings were spread wide in an imitation of flight as it turned slowly in the freezing air.

The boggart's head jerked up suddenly. With a hiss, it loped back off along the tunnel towards the drain, the fur along its spine bristling. The hob knew without a doubt that the crawling man had caught up with them.

'Make the crawly thing go away,' Curious breathed, his voice shaking with terror.

The hob pushed Curious towards the pile of mouldering cloths. 'We have to hide.' *Though much good it will do us if the crawly man defeats the boggart*, he thought, but he kept this to himself. Curious was terrified enough as it was.

The cloth smelled sour with damp. The hob saw stitches of tarnished gold thread and a memory stirred deep in his mind. He had seen cloths like this before, carefully stored in a chest in a room near the abbey church. Back then, the cloths were white and the gold thread shone like glints of sunshine. The brother men would be sad to see them like this.

The hob crouched down. Beside him, Curious began to whisper: '*Et dimitte nobis debita nostra sicut et nos dimittimus debitoribus nostris. Et ne nos inducas in tentationem, sed libera nos a malo.*'

'What do the words mean?' the hob asked.

'I don't know, but the monks used to say them. I think they are magic words.'

The brother men had no time for magic, the hob knew, but he said nothing.

'*Sed libera nos a malo*,' Curious murmured again, huddling as close to the hob as he could.

The boggart let out a screech that almost made the hob jump out of his fur. His heart thumped wildly as he listened to claws scrabbling on stone and the splash of something heavy moving through water. A yowl echoed along the drain, followed by snarling and more splashing. The hob clutched Curious and held him tightly. Beneath his scarf, the little hob was shaking like a twig in a gale.

'Quickly! Say more of the brother men's words,' the hob urged.

'*Et ne nos inducas in tentation!*' Curious gabbled as he gripped pawfuls of the hob's fur. '*Sed libera nos a malo!*'

Above the boggart's screeches rose another sound, a howl of rage that vibrated through the drain and tunnel. The sound faded away and a tense silence followed. The hob could barely breathe from the terror clawing at his body. Then he heard grunting and snuffling as something splashed along the stream, heading towards the lair. It *sounded* like the boggart.

The hob peered cautiously around the cloths and to his relief, saw the boggart appear at the far end of the tunnel. It sat there for a while, peering back along the drain, the white lantern light glinting on its fur. It scratched its belly and huffed great cloudy breaths into the cold air. As far as the hob could see, the creature was none the worse for its encounter with the crawling man.

'I think the boggart sent it away,' the hob whispered.

'Did the magic words help?' Curious asked hopefully.

The hob nodded. 'They most likely did, yes.'

The boggart loped along the tunnel and climbed over the wall by the entrance to its lair. It squatted in the middle of the floor and stroked the handle of a basket full of broken tiles protectively. Keeping a wary eye on the creature, the hob stepped out from his hiding place. Now that the danger had passed, would the boggart decide it was hungry and in need of a hob-sized morsel to eat?

Curious crawled out from behind the cloths and got to his feet. This was hampered by the scarf, which had loosened and was now tangled around his legs. He pulled it free and straightened up. 'Has the crawly thing gone forever?'

The boggart grunted and shifted on its haunches. It jerked its head to one side.

Curious's shoulders drooped. 'He said no.' He took a few hesitant steps forward, one end of the wet and muddy scarf trailing behind him. The boggart watched him closely.

'What are you *doing*?' the hob said anxiously. 'Come *back*!'

Curious took no notice. He stood in front of the boggart and reached out to pat the creature's knee. 'Brave thing. Very, *very* brave.'

The boggart huffed and looked away, then glanced back at Curious. It peered around, as if searching for something. The hob watched in surprise as the creature picked up a dead worm, pale and bloated, from a puddle. It dangled from a sharp claw as the boggart held it out to the small hob.

Curious took the worm and stared at it for several moments. He looked at the hob and whispered, 'What is it?'

'A worm, an earth creature,' the hob said.

The boggart ran its tongue over its lips and grunted.

'I *think*...the boggart means for you to eat it.'

Curious inspected the worm and wrinkled his nose. He shook it and it flopped limply. 'Do I have to?'

'We do not want to offend the boggart, in case it gets angry. Maybe you could just take a small nibble?'

Curious licked the worm cautiously. With obvious reluctance, he took a bite from it and chewed it slowly. 'It's not very nice,' he said at last.

The boggart reached out and took the rest of the worm from him. It sucked out the insides, and then chewed on the skin. The hob watched in horrified fascination. He liked worms; they were busy creatures who kept the earth alive. Sometimes they found their way into his burrow. They were good company, even if they had very little to say for themselves. He would *never* eat one, puddle drowned or not.

It must be almost dusk, the hob suddenly thought. *Ned and the men will be leaving the abbey soon. Perhaps we could leave with the boy tonight and come back to the abbey tomorrow, just in case the crawly man comes after us again?* 'Curious, we have to go to the yard *now*,' he said. 'The boy Ned is taking us home with him, on his cart. But thank you,' he added hurriedly, looking up at the boggart, 'for saving us from the crawly man.'

The boggart picked bits of worm skin from between its teeth and grunted. It loped off along the tunnel, towards the drain, and waited for the hobs to follow it before jumping down into the stream.

Hurrying after the boggart, the hob gasped as he stepped into the freezing water. Curious was close behind him, his teeth chattering loudly. The hob carefully sidestepped the bones as he waded back along the drain. *Whose bones are they?* he wondered. *Did the boggart have anything to do with them being there?*

The boggart climbed out of the drain and reached down to pull the hob up after him, setting him on the icy cobbles with a bump.

The hob stared around at the silent, empty yard in dismay. 'Oh, no, no! We are too late,' he said. 'They left without us!'

It was already dusk and the carts had gone.

Chapter Eleven

The hob knew they could not risk sleeping in the barn. He had the unsettling feeling that they were being watched. There was a nastiness in the air which warned him that the crawling man was close by. The boggart had saved them once but they might not be so lucky a second time. He took Curious to the ash tree where he had kept watch for the Deerman and they settled on a sturdy branch, their backs against the trunk. They huddled together for warmth, wrapped in the scarf, but the autumn night was as bitter as death. Frost crackled in the air and covered every twig, branch and fallen leaf in the forest with ice; it coated the scarf and glistened on the ends of the hobs' fur in the moonlight.

The hob slept in short snatches. He passed the long night watching the stars travel slowly across the sky. Beside him, Curious whispered in his sleep from time to time. The hob recognised the brother men's magic words. It seemed strange to think that the only creature in the abbey who would ever speak them again was a hob.

The night passed peacefully. The Deerman did not appear and nor did the crawling man. Nothing disturbed the frozen silence until dawn streaked the eastern sky with bands of pink and gold, and the rooks roosting in the forest began to caw.

'The carts will be here soon,' the hob said, stretching his cold limbs. 'Ned will bring us some food and we can go back to the barn and sleep.'

'Good,' Curious whispered. 'I think I have turned back to stone.'

The hob watched for the first glimpse of the carts. He heard them at last, the sound of wheels grating over frozen ruts.

'They are here!' He threw the scarf to the ground. It would just get in the way as they climbed down from the tree. 'Quickly, follow me.'

The hob clambered from branch to branch, nimble and sure footed, but Curious followed more slowly, whimpering softly as he felt with his feet for toeholds on the icy branches.

'Wait! Wait for me, Brother Walter!' the small hob called anxiously. 'Don't leave me behind!'

Curious missed his footing on the lowest branch and landed beside the hob with a grunt. The hob helped him to his feet and wrapped the scarf around him again. They hid behind a knot of brambles to wait until the carts had turned onto the causeway and were trundling towards the gatehouse before running after them. By the time they reached the yard, the men were already inside the church and the sound of hammers on stone echoed on the frosty air.

The hob led Curious up to the loft in the barn and they settled in their nests. For a while, the hob slept. He woke to the smell of beer and cheese and bread. He crept from his nest and peered over the edge of the loft. Something was wrong. The men were sitting around the small fire on the stone hearth, eating their midday meal in silence.

Glancing up, Ned saw him and tried to smile, but his mouth would not let him. The boy was scared, the hob realised. What had happened?

The men stayed in the barn for longer than usual. They seemed reluctant to leave the fire and go back to work. They glanced fearfully towards the barn door from time to time and the hob saw Kit take a sprig of mistletoe from inside his jerkin and hold it in his fist. Tobias glanced at him with a frown.

'What's *that* for?'

'It wards off evil,' Kit said, lifting his chin defiantly, as if daring the older man to mock him. 'Jack Thatcher gave it to me t' other day.'

'Didn't do *him* much good,' Tobias muttered. He sucked the beer from the bristly tails of his moustache and belched. 'Pardon me.'

Kit's cheeks reddened. 'Well, I ain't taking any chances.'

'Ye'll need more than a twig of mistletoe to keep ye safe,' Tobias said, a hard edge to his voice. His dark eyebrows drew together in a fierce frown. He took a stick and jabbed the fire, sending sparks scattering upwards.

Noll picked up his basket and beer jug and got to his feet. 'No point in puttin' it off any longer. We've work to do.'

The hob watched the others gather their belongings together, moving reluctantly. Noll waited by the door as Ned and Kit left the barn. He took Tobias's arm and held him back.

'Ye know Sir Samuel is just lookin' for an excuse to put yer family out of yer house,' Noll said. 'Without this work, ye won't be able to pay yer rent, and ye know that.'

'Of course I know that, but what's happenin' here is bad, Noll,' Tobias said angrily. He pulled off his cap and scratched his scalp, his fingers rummaging through the thick black hair as they chased nits. Peering down from the hayloft, the hob thought he looked more like the boggart than ever. 'If ye'd asked me if I believed in ghosts afore we came to work here, like that soft-witted Jack Thatcher, I'd have laughed at ye, but now...' He shook his head and pulled on his cap. 'That...*thing* we seen in the church this morning, that crawlin' horror, d'ye know what I think?'

Noll folded his arms. His expression was grim as he met Tobias's gaze. 'Ye think it's what's left of the king's man who hanged Abbot Matthew, don't ye?'

The hob saw the look that went between the two men. They were frightened but there was something more; he had seen the same look on Ned's face. There were secrets here.

'It *is* him,' Tobias said softly, 'and he's come for us, Noll. He's come to get his revenge. We can't stay here.'

103

'Ye want to be the one to tell Sir Samuel why we ain't doin' the work he's payin' us for?' Noll's voice was gruff. 'And maybe we should tell him who killed the king's man while we're at it.'

'Shh! Quiet!' Tobias hissed. 'We don't speak 'bout that, *ever*.' He glanced around nervously, as if fearing he might be overheard.

'Best get back to the church,' Noll said. 'We're safer stayin' all together.'

Tobias spat on the floor. 'Ain't none of us safe and ye know it, long as we're in this God forsaken place.'

The hob squatted by the edge of the loft long after the men had gone, thinking about what they had said. He remembered what Urchin had told him about the men who had beaten the king's man to death with flails and sticks, as punishment for hanging the abbot. Had Tobias and Noll been amongst them?

Did Ned know the truth?

Sadness as soft as a whisper settled over the hob. He liked Ned's father, but taking a life was a terrible thing to do, a *wrong* thing. If the king's man was evil for killing the abbot, then what did that make Noll Swyfte?

The hob wrapped his arms around his body. He felt weary to the bone and very old. Human lives were filled with so much hurt and unhappiness. They did such bad things to each other and to the creatures around them. Their moments of kindness and goodness were all too often swept away by a dark flood of evil, and even the best of them sometimes cast a long shadow.

The hob had a sudden longing to be back in the forest, where life was so much simpler. He knew that if the Deerman came to the abbey now, at this moment, he would take Curious and follow the creature to the forest without a backward glance. And then he felt ashamed of himself. Urchin was just a lonely, lost child, and the old pig had never harmed another creature. To leave them behind would make him as heartless as a human.

'I'm a *hob*,' he whispered fiercely to himself, 'and a hob does not turn his back on a friend.'

With that, he settled in his nest again and let his dreams take him back to the forest.

***

That afternoon, Ned came to find the hob.

'Ye there, little Walter?' he called softly from below the hayloft.

The hob looked over the edge of the loft. 'Yes.'

Ned smiled up at him. 'I was worried when ye didn't turn up yestere'en. Was hoping ye'd come home with us.'

The hob climbed down the ladder and sat on a hearthstone. Ned took a leather pouch from inside his jerkin and handed it to him. 'Brought these for ye.'

The hob took the pouch and opened it. Inside were the biggest, fattest hazelnuts he had ever seen. They had been cracked from their shells and roasted over a fire. 'You are a very kind human,' he said, grinning widely. He tipped the nuts onto a stone and divided them into two even piles, one for him, one for Curious. While he ate, he told Ned what had happened yesterday. The boy listened in shocked silence.

'So the boggart ain't evil, then?' Ned said when he had finished. 'He saved ye?'

The hob nodded. 'I thought it was chasing me the other night, but it was trying to warn me about the crawling thing,' the hob said, stuffing a nut into his mouth.

'Tobias saw someone watching us from down near the West Door this mornin', all grey and tattered, kneeling on the floor. Gave 'im a right scare, it did,' he said, frowning. 'Gave us *all* a right scare.'

'The crawly man,' the hob said. He paused for a moment and then decided the time to keep secrets had passed. 'He is after your father and Tobias.'

'What d'ye mean?'

The hob gave him a level stare. 'I think you know.'

Ned's cheeks flushed and his eyes were bright with tears. He knelt down by the hearth and bowed his head. 'My father's a *good* man, and Tobias too. They didn't mean to *kill* the king's man, they were just angry when they found the abbot hanging from the gate

106

arch.' His voice choked in his throat and a tear splashed onto a hearthstone, a dark star in the wood ash. 'Abbot Matthew was well liked in the villages. He was always the first to help when harvests failed or people weren't able to feed their families. He would open up the abbey barns to feed them. He didn't deserve to die like that. The king's men took everything of any worth from the abbey, right down to the lead from the windows, but they were greedy. They thought Abbot Matthew was hiding treasure and they didn't want to leave without it.'

'But they never found it,' the hob said.

'No, they didn't.' Ned hunched forward, his dark hair flopping across his face. He sniffed and wiped his nose on the sleeve of his doublet. 'I was supposed to be asleep in the loft when my father came home that night, five years ago. I heard him tell Mam that the king's men had turned the monks out onto the road, but they kept the abbot and one of the monks behind, to try and find out where the abbey treasure was hid. My father cried.' Ned stopped and wiped his eyes. 'Ain't never seen him do that, ever. He said they tortured the two monks, and then hanged Abbot Matthew. Mam heard me moving about and told my father to hush, and they never spoke about it again in my hearing. But I saw him, Brother Walter, that night he came home from the abbey, his clothes all stained with blood... I was only eight years old and too young to know what it was all about, but I know *now*.'

The hob sat quietly and waited for the boy to continue. He ached with pity for him. The hurt of what his father had done would live with him for a long, long time.

Ned got to his feet and walked to the barn door. He stood with his shoulders hunched against the cold, staring out across the yard. 'Word reached the village that the leader of the king's men had gone missing. People said he found the treasure and made off with it, but that ain't what happened. He's buried somewhere in the abbey, and now, if what ye say is right, his ghost is coming after my father and Tobias.'

The hob remembered the bones he had stumbled over on the way to the boggart's lair. 'I saw bones in the drain yesterday. I think they might have belonged to the crawly man.'

Ned turned to stare at him. 'And the treasure? Was it there with him?'

The hob shook his head.

'We *have* to leave the abbey,' Ned said anxiously, 'but my father don't want to cross Sir Samuel. He ain't a nice man; ye don't want to make *him* angry. Nobody can stand up to him, because he's a powerful man and we are just...plain folk. Ye ain't goin' to tell anyone, are ye? About my father and Tobias?'

Who would listen to a hob, even supposing they could see me? the hob thought. *And what would be gained by it anyway?* 'No.'

A rustling came from overhead. 'My middle bit is growling again,' Curious said sleepily, his face appearing over the edge of the loft.

The hob pointed to the remaining pile of nuts. 'These are yours.'

'I have to go,' Ned said. 'Tomorrow's Sunday so we ain't working here, but it's also the eve of the feast of St Francis, the day when the old Cold Fair used to start. It lasted three days and the ghost fair can show itself any time over those days, so it's said. I can take ye up to the fair field, if ye really mean to go. Just make sure ye're on the cart when we leave.'

The hob nodded. 'Thank you.'

Curious climbed down to sit by the embers of the fire. He peered around warily as he ate his hazelnuts. 'My fur is prickly,' he whispered.

'Mine too,' the hob said. He sensed danger, close and threatening. The atmosphere in the barn was changing. The shadows seemed a little darker, the air colder. Any thought of returning to his nest to doze away the afternoon was forgotten.

The hob gathered up the last of the nuts. 'We will finish these in the church, and stay close to the men and their carts until they leave. We do not want to be left behind again.'

Curious took his acorn with him, and the hob brought his star-painted wood. They slipped through the West Door of the church and hid behind a pillar in the south aisle. From here, the hob could see Noll and Tobias working at the top of the scaffolding, while Ned and Kit piled stones onto handcarts.

The gaping hole where the north transept used to be let the daylight into the nave and meant there was no shelter from the biting cold. The hob could not get warm. The sky above the roofless church was as blue as a snow shadow and the air tingled with frost. Cold struck up from the tiled floor, numbing his feet and haunches. Beside him, Curious was bundled up and shivering inside his scarf.

To wile away the time, the hob ran his finger over the patterns painted on the pillar and hummed softly. Curious began to sing one of the brother men's songs in a little warbling voice. The hob clapped a paw over his mouth and whispered, '*Sshh!*'

Curious squatted in miserable silence and picked at a loose thread on his scarf. Before long, he had unravelled a tangle of yarn. He stared at it in confusion. 'What's happening, Brother Walter?' he whispered. 'Why is my scoff turning to a scriffle?'

The hob broke the yarn close to the scarf and tucked the end into the knitting. 'There. Now, do not pick at any more threads or you'll have no scarf at all.'

Curious sighed and rested his cheek on his updrawn knees, and stared off into the distance.

The hob's fur began to bristle again. The air in the church felt heavy, as if a storm was coming. He peered around the pillar and gasped in horror; a ragged grey figure was moving across the nave from the direction of the West Door. It crawled on its hands and knees, its face lifted towards the men on the scaffolding. The white eyes in the withered face were sunken pools of malevolence. Through the trailing rags, the hob glimpsed twisted and broken legs, and bones poking through withered flesh.

Ned was emptying rubble from one of the baskets, which Noll had lowered on a rope from the top of the scaffolding. Neither he nor Kit had noticed the danger creeping towards them. The hob waved his arms frantically to catch his attention. Ned glanced around and the hob pointed to the crawling man.

'There! *There!*' the hob mouthed, jigging up and down on the spot, fur hackling, tail twitching. Curious whimpered and grabbed the hob's leg.

Ned yelped in fear and dropped the basket. Startled, Kit turned around to see what was happening and then panic broke out, with Ned and Kit shouting and shoving each other out of the way in their desperation to escape. Noll and Tobias looked over the edge of the scaffolding. Tobias stumbled backwards with a yell of terror, dropping his hammer and chisel. They clattered down to the ground, narrowly missing Kit's head.

The crawling man reached the scaffolding and wrapped bony fingers around the first strut.

'Get down from there!' Ned screamed up at his father. 'He's coming for ye!'

Noll and Tobias began to climb down as fast as they could. The scaffolding creaked and started to sway. Kit and Ned ducked out of the way of falling hammers, stones and planks of wood, arms shielding their heads.

The hob saw the look of horror on the Ned's face as he watched the crawling man haul itself upright, hand over hand. With inhuman strength, it rocked the strut hard and the two men lost their footing. Yelling in terror, they fell to the ground with the scaffolding collapsing around them.

Noll landed heavily and rolled onto his back, groaning.

'Father!' Ned shouted, lunging forwards. He leaned over his father to shield him from the scaffolding struts clattering down around them. Tobias lay nearby, not moving, and the hob saw immediately that the man's leg was broken. It lay twisted with the foot pointing in the wrong direction. Kit darted forward to drag him out of harm's way.

In the silence that followed, the terrified men stared around but there was no sign of the crawling horror. Broken struts and planks lay scattered over the nave and stone and plaster dust coiled on the air. Ned helped his father to sit up. The hob saw Noll cradling his arm to his chest, his face twisted in pain, coughing as the gritty dust caught in his throat. He struggled to his feet, supported by a white-faced Ned and limped over to where Tobias lay. 'Is he alive?'

'Just about,' Kit said in a shaking voice. 'His leg's broke.' He stared around, his eyes bulging with terror. 'Did ye see it? *Did ye?* Noll, we got to get away from here *now*!'

'Enough is enough.' Noll's voice was hoarse. 'We're goin' back to Yagleah and we ain't coming here again. Sir Samuel can do what he likes 'bout that. Get Tobias settled on a cart and fetch the tools.'

Ned and Kit struggled to lift Tobias onto a handcart. Kit wheeled him out to the yard while Ned hurriedly gathered up the tools. Noll walked to the West Door, moving slowly and stiffly. The hob was sure he had hurt more than his arm.

'We have to leave too,' the hob said anxiously to Curious.

Curious bundled up the remains of his scarf and followed the hob to the door. Nobody noticed them climb onto the back of Noll's cart and hide behind the baskets of rubble and stone. They were all too busy getting Tobias settled comfortably on the other cart and loading the tools before the crawling man reappeared. Kit and Ned led the horses from the pasture and harnessed them to the carts. The animals sensed their fear and became restless. The hob heard them stamping and snorting.

'Steady, steady,' Kit said, but there was an edge of panic to his voice. 'We'll be away from here soon enough. Steady, Sampson.'

The hob jumped when someone peered over the side of the cart but it was only Ned. The boy nodded and looked relieved to see them, then disappeared again. Through a gap in the baskets, the hob saw Ned help his father up onto the seat board before climbing up beside him. With a flick of the reins, they set off after Kit's cart.

The hob's teeth rattled as the carts trundled across the cobbles.

'My bones are loose,' Curious whispered. 'They're moving around inside my fur. They might fall *out*.' He wedged himself into a corner but this only made matters worse. He held his jaws shut with his paws and hummed softly and anxiously, the sound quavering in time with the jolting of the cart.

As they passed under the gatehouse arch, the hob peered through a gap in the baskets and saw the boggart squatting beside the hole in the drain, a forlorn look on its face as it watched them go. None of the Yagleah men noticed it.

'We've left the smelly thing behind,' Curious whispered sadly, waving a paw. 'Goodbye.'

The hob felt sorry for the creature but it could not come with them; boggarts did not live well with humans.

'I think it can take care of itself,' the hob said, 'and it has magic to help it.'

Ned stopped the cart on the bridge and ran back to close the gate. The hob saw the boggart clamber down into the drain and he sensed the creature's loneliness. Just when the boggart thought he had found a friend, he was being abandoned.

We will be back, the hob said silently, *I promise*. He did not know if the boggart heard him but a long quavering yowl came from the drain.

'What was *that*?' Kit turned to stare back at the abbey, white-faced with horror.

'Just a fox,' Noll called. 'Probably. Ned, hurry, boy. The more distance we put between us and this cursed place, the happier I'll be.'

'Amen to that!' Kit called. 'And we *ain't* coming back!'

Chapter Twelve

The hob wrapped himself in a sack to keep warm on the journey to Yagleah. Beside him, Curious peered through a gap in the wattle sides of the cart. His eyes were wide with awe as he stared out at the flood meadows and river, the forest and the wide sweep of blue sky.

'I didn't know the world was so *big*, Brother Walter,' he murmured.

'It is a very big place indeed,' the hob agreed. 'You can walk for *days* and still not reach the edge of it.'

By midday, the carts were within sight of Yagleah. It was a long time since the hob had travelled this way. He gazed out at half remembered fields and woods, and suddenly thought of an old friend, an elf, dead these many years, who had lived in an ancient burial mound near the village. An idea started to take shape in his mind. He shuffled down to the end of the cart, where he sat and watched for the mound. *There!* Overgrown now with thorn trees but unmistakably the place where the elf had lived. He thought with mingled affection and sadness of his friend and the happy times they had spent together.

Other memories of this place were darker; he remembered a time of death, two hundred years ago, when the forest fays had been hunted down and slaughtered by the Dark King of the Unseelie Court and his fay warriors. He had taken shelter with the elf several times, when the fighting came too close. His heart beat a little faster at the memory of the battle in the forest, when a great hero had risen up to fight the Dark King. He had lost good friends during those terrible days. The old elf was just one amongst many.

'What are you looking at?' Curious asked, coming to sit beside him.

The hob pointed to the mound. 'That. Underneath it is the home of an elf I used to be friends with but it's empty now. I was thinking, perhaps it would make a new lair for the boggart.'

'What about his treasure?'

'There is plenty of room for it, and there is gold in the mound for him to guard, along with the bones of a human warrior from a time long ago. I think the boggart will like that.'

The carts followed the road up the rise of a low hill. To one side there was a ditch with a bank and hedge just beyond it. Not for the first time, the hob puzzled over the human need to build walls and fences to close away part of the land. Whoever dug the ditch and planted the hedge was saying *this is mine*. The hob shook his head sadly. Nobody owned the land or the sky, or the stars, the moon, the rivers and trees. Humans believed all of it was theirs to do with as they pleased, and that made his heart ache.

The carts reached a fork in the road and Ned stopped his cart beside Kit's.

'I'll send word up to Master Dunch at the new build,' Noll said, his face grey with pain, 'and tell him we won't be working at the abbey anymore. *He* can tell his lordship.'

Kit nodded but he looked worried. 'What if Sir Samuel decides to punish us by turnin' us out of our houses, Noll?'

'Then we'll all go and live with Jack Thatcher,' Noll said with an attempt at a smile.

Kit pulled a face. 'Think I'd sooner live in the hedgerow. I'll come by and see ye later, but I'd best take Tobias home now.'

Noll nodded. 'How is he?

'His leg's still broke, but he's woken up, so that's a good sign.' An arm waved feebly from the back of the cart.

'I'll send Bess Pollkin to him,' Noll said. 'She'll mend him, if anyone can.'

Kit nodded and flicked Sampson's reins. 'Walk on, boy.' The cart turned off along a road leading uphill towards a row of houses.

Is Bess Pollkin Ned's mam's sister, the same Bess who likes hobs? the hob wondered. *If she is the same person, then she is a healer like Brother Snail was. I think I will like her.*

'On ye go, Flit!' Ned called. The horse plodded towards the village green and out of long habit, turned off along a lane leading to a timber and wattle house in the lee of the hill. They reached a yard beyond a hawthorn hedge and the cart came to a standstill. A plump, brown-haired woman and several small children came out of the

118

house, while two men and a young boy emerged from a large shed on the other side of the yard. The hob saw their shocked expressions when they saw Noll's injuries.

'Noll!' the woman cried. 'What's happened to ye?'

'Let's get 'im inside first, Mam, questions can wait,' one of the men called. Sawdust powdered his dark hair and he looked like an older version of Ned. 'Give us a hand, Thomas.'

An old man, his face a mazy web of wrinkles beneath a leather cap, hurried across the yard to help Noll from the cart.

'Lean on Edmund,' Thomas said as he guided one of Noll's feet to the top of the cart wheel. Edmund, the dark-haired young man, reached up and took Noll's good arm.

'John, unharness Flit, and feed and water him,' Edmund called over his shoulder. A boy ran forward and started to unbuckle the harness straps. 'Ned, run and fetch Bess.'

The hob waited until everyone had gone inside and Tom had led the horse away. He helped Curious down from the cart and together, they slipped into the house behind Ned's family.

A stone-flagged passageway led from the front to the back of the building. Light and the sound of voices came from an open doorway to the left. A second door, across the passage, was closed.

'Stay close,' the hob whispered to Curious. They crept forward cautiously and the hob looked around the edge of the door frame. The shuttered windows kept out the afternoon light along with the autumn chill. The room was lit by two lanterns and the fire burning on the hearth of a huge stone fireplace. A ladder led up to a loft below the roof rafters. A long oak table, with benches and stools and a high-backed chair, took up one half of the room. Plain oak cupboards and chests crowded the other half, and what little space was left seemed to be filled with people, tall, small, all talking and shouting at once.

Grabbing Curious by the paw, the hob scurried across to a cupboard and crouched down in the dark corner beyond it. He propped his piece of painted wood against the wall. The golden stars glowed softly in the lantern light, a small patch of peace in the noisy chaos of Ned's home.

Curious, worn out by the uncomfortable cart ride, curled up inside the tattered remains of his scarf and fell into an exhausted sleep. The family bustled around Noll. Two of the smaller children cried loudly, while Mam and Edmund helped Noll off with his jerkin, easing it carefully over his broken arm. The hob was so intent on watching them that, at first, he did not see a woman kneeling in front of the fire, heating an iron poker in the embers. He jumped when he heard her gasp. The woman's eyes widened in astonishment and she knelt quite still. The hob saw a strong resemblance to Ned and his mam in her thin face but her eyes were blue and the hair beneath her linen cap was fair. There were deep creases by the corners of her eyes.

This is a face that likes to smile, he thought, though she was not smiling now.

The hob held his breath and waited to see what she would do. Hit him with the poker, maybe? Scream?

The poker slipped from her fingers and clattered onto the hearthstones. Hurriedly she snatched it up and pushed it back into the fire. She glanced at him again, blinked, and then looked away. The hob saw her take a deep breath and stare into the flames for a few moments.

'Ned,' she called evenly, 'come here.'

Ned knelt down beside her. He saw the hob and he grinned.

'Look in that corner,' the woman said softly. She sounded calm but the hob saw that her hands were trembling. 'D'ye see a small hairy creature that ain't a cat or a dog?'

Ned nodded.

'Would ye know owt about it? How it got there, mebbe?'

Again, Ned nodded. 'Told ye they were real, Bess, didn't I?'

Bess looked at him sharply. 'Them? Ye brought *more* back with ye?'

'Just one, and he's only little.'

'I see.' She took the poker from the fire and dipped it into the jug standing on the hearth nearby. Steam hissed and there was a smell of apples.

She stood up and carried the jug of mulled cider to the table, where she filled a cup and put it in front of Noll. He leaned on the table with his good elbow. The bruises on his face were an angry blue-black and his broken arm rested in a linen sling. One of the children, a girl about Ned's age, lifted the cup of cider to her father's mouth and with a brief smile, he lowered his head to drink.

'Stand aside, all of ye,' Bess said. 'Let me look at ye, Noll, and see what ye've done to yerself.'

Ned turned to the hob and whispered, 'Ye better hide, and stay hid this time.'

The hob huddled behind the cupboard and wondered what Bess was going to do. She could see him, which was a rare thing. He knew from Ned that there had been a hob in her father's house when she was a girl but he could not tell if she was pleased to find herself in the company of two more. *I hope her hob was well behaved and that she hasn't forgotten it.*

He sat and worried while Bess tended to Noll. At last the room quietened down and the younger children were sent from the house to give Noll some peace. To his surprise and delight, a dish of milk and a piece of freshly baked bread appeared on the floor beside the cupboard. The hob glimpsed Bess's hand as she pushed the bowl towards him. A warm glow started somewhere deep inside his chest and spread through his body. She *liked* hobs! He left Curious to sleep but kept a share of the bread and milk for him to have later.

At last, with a full belly and sure in the knowledge that he and Curious were safe enough for now, he lay down and slept.

***

The sound of voices woke the hob. He rubbed his eyes and stretched. Curious was already awake and eating his bread. He held a crust out to the hob. 'Would you like some?' he whispered.

'That's yours,' the hob said, 'I've eaten mine.'

'My scoff has gone,' Curious said. 'It must have scriffled away.'

Been taken, more likely, and thrown away, the hob thought. He would need to find something to keep Curious warm before they went out in the cold again. This weather was not friendly to hobs and it was not even winter yet.

Noll sat at the table with Kit, Ned and Edmund. The lantern light turned their faces to masks of gold and shadows. Ned's mam sat in a chair by the hearth, mending a linen undershirt by firelight.

'So what did Master Dunch say when ye told him we ain't going back to the abbey?' Noll asked. He looked old that evening, as if the events of the day had aged him. His greying hair hung in limp hanks around his face and he sat hunched over, as if his stomach hurt. There was pain in his eyes and in his voice.

123

'He didn't seem too surprised, but then Sir Samuel rode by to see how his new build was going, and when Master Dunch told him what had happened, he were so angry I thought he'd burst his belly.' Kit shook his head. 'Said we were a bunch of work shy, idle...' he glanced at Ned's mam and cleared his throat, 'well, it don't matter what he said we were, but he said the abbey *ain't* haunted, 'cause there ain't any such thing as ghosts.'

'Knows that for a fact, does he?' Noll said angrily. The hob could see a thin piece of wood, bound up with linen strips, holding his broken arm bone in place. 'Maybe he'd like to go and take a look for himself.'

'Or perhaps he'd like to take a stroll up to the fair field tomorrow, and let's see what he has to say about ghosts *then*,' Edmund said. 'That'll sort him out, *right* good.'

'There ain't a ghost fair.' Noll frowned down into his cup. 'That's just an old story.'

Kit's eyes narrowed. 'Ye said the ghost at the abbey were just a story too, till ye saw it for yerself.'

Noll's cheeks flushed. 'That's different.'

'Don't see how,' Kit said.

The men finished their cider in silence.

'Master Dunch'll be coming by to see ye in the morning,' Kit said as he got up to leave.

124

Noll frowned. 'I ain't goin' back to the abbey for him nor anyone else.'

'He ain't like Sir Samuel,' Tobias said, wrapping a scarf around his neck. 'I think he *knows*.'

Noll snorted. 'So what's he coming by for?'

'Maybe to pay ye?' Ned's mam said. The steward always dealt with such matters for Sir Samuel.

'I won't be holding my breath, Agnes, and nor should ye.'

After Kit set out into the freezing night, Agnes covered the fire and the family went off to their beds. Ned and Edmund climbed the ladder to the loft, while Noll and Agnes went to the parlour across the passageway.

The hob waited until the household had settled and all was quiet before going to sit by the hearth. He struggled to lift the heavy earthenware *couvre feu* aside and warmed his paws over the embers. Curious sat beside him.

The hobs sat in companionable silence as around them the timber bones of the house creaked and settled. *Tomorrow I will look for the fair,* the hob thought, *but for now, it is good to be warm and safe, with a full belly and new friends.*

Curious sighed and curled up on the hearth. Firelight danced in his sleepy golden eyes. 'I wish I was brave like you,' he whispered.

The hob smiled. 'I am not brave. I try to be but I am just a hob.'

125

'A very *brave* hob.'

Chapter Thirteen

The household began to stir at dawn. The hobs hid behind the cupboard until the family had finished their very noisy morning meal and the older ones had left the house to start their chores. Agnes bundled up the youngest children in warm clothing and they followed the others outside. Ned came to find the hobs.

'Bess gave me this for Curious,' he said, holding up an old woollen tunic, small enough for a human baby. The hob took it and saw that it was just the right size for Curious. No more trailing scarves and unravelling yarn. He helped Curious to put it on.

'It will keep you warm until your winter fur grows,' the hob said.

Curious smiled in delight and stroked the wool, his fingers finding the neat little patches where it had been darned.

'Ye look splendid,' Ned said with a grin.

Curious nodded in agreement.

'I got a cart load of wattle hurdles to take to Bereton Mill before church. The mill's a short way past the abbey, so I'll be gone till mid- morning,' Ned said.

'But what about the Cold Fair?' the hob asked.

'We'll go up to the field later. There ain't any rush, 'cause it could be there any time these next three days, or it might not be there at all. Ain't no way of knowin' until we get there.'

The hob had no choice but to be satisfied with this. He turned his attention to the problem of the boggart. He quickly explained his idea of moving the boggart and its treasure to the old burial mound.

Ned looked troubled. 'That would mean us going back to the abbey to fetch him.'

'It will not be able to carry all its treasure to the mound,' the hob said. 'There is too much and I don't think it'll want to leave any behind.'

'Ye want me to take it all on the cart, don't ye?' Ned said, but it wasn't a question. 'After what happened yesterday, my father will be angry if he finds out I've gone anywhere near the abbey again.'

The hob hunched his shoulders and looked dejectedly into the fire. He would just have to find a way to do this on his own. It wasn't fair to expect Ned to risk his life just to rescue a smelly old boggart.

'Very well,' Ned said reluctantly, 'we'll stop at the abbey on our way back from the mill. We can pile his treasure on the cart, but we have to be quick about it. I ain't staying a moment longer than I have to. Just a pity he ain't found the abbey treasure, 'cause we could have fetched that too, but if we don't know where it's hid...'

'Perhaps the monks put it in the wall with the box,' Curious said, stroking the worn wool of his tunic. His tail was curled around the golden acorn, lying on the floor beside him.

'Box? What box?' the hob said. 'What wall?'

Curious glanced up, his eyes widening at the fierce look on the hob's face. 'In the cloister alley. Just before the monks left the abbey and never came back, two of them took the door off a cupboard in the wall and put a box inside, then made a new bit of wall with some stones to hide it.'

The hob looked at Ned and saw the excitement in the boy's eyes.

'The treasure!' Ned breathed. 'It has to be.'

The hob turned back to Curious. 'Can you show us where the box is hidden?'

Curious nodded. 'I...I think so.'

'I'll go and harness Flit,' Ned said, scrambling to his feet. 'Meet me in the yard.'

'What will we do with the treasure if we find it?' the hob called after him.

'Don't know, but it ain't going to end up in Sir Samuel's hands, *that's* for sure.' And with that, Ned was gone.

'We're not going to stay at the abbey, are we?' Curious asked anxiously. 'Can't we stay here? I *like* it here.'

The hob patted his shoulder. 'We will not be at the abbey for long, and then we'll come back.'

'But what about the crawly thing?' Curious said.

'We will be long gone before it knows we were even there,' the hob said with more certainty than he felt. The look on the small hob's face told him he wasn't convinced.

The hob hid his painted wood in the gap between the cupboard and the wall, and then set off after Ned. Curious followed him, clutching his acorn, and they left the house.

There was nobody in the yard apart from Ned. He stood by the shed door talking to somebody inside. The hob heard children somewhere beyond the yard, shrieking and laughing, and glimpsed Agnes walking between two sheds, carrying a basket.

The hobs settled themselves behind the hurdles on the back of the cart. Ned climbed onto the seat board. He glanced over his shoulder at them and nodded.

'Hup, Flit,' he called, jiggling the reins. The cart lurched, the stack of hurdles creaked, and they left the yard.

Low cloud and an uneasy wind had banished the frosty cold, leaving a misty autumn day in its place. When the cart was safely away from the village, the hob and Curious climbed up to sit beside Ned. Seeing the passing fields and woods from so high up made an interesting change, the hob thought. He sniffed the air contentedly. He had missed the feel of the wind in his fur and the smell of earth and old leaves, good *foresty* smells.

They rode past the turning to the abbey and followed a lane alongside the river to the mill. The hobs hid beneath an empty sack on the back of the cart while Ned and the miller's son unloaded the hurdles. The miller counted out the coins in payment, and Ned and the hobs were soon on their way again. The hob waited until they were out of the mill yard before sitting up beside the boy again.

The hob's carefree mood lasted until they turned onto the causeway to the abbey. Ned stopped the cart near the bridge and went to open the gate. *It looks*, the hob thought, *like a mouth, waiting to swallow us whole.* The cart trundled under the gate arch and into the yard. The noise of the wheels on the cobbles brought the boggart clambering up through the hole in the drain. It huffed and slapped the ground and seemed delighted to see them. Ned sat and stared at the creature, his face frozen with shock.

'That's the boggart,' the hob said as he helped Curious down from the cart. 'It won't harm you.'

Ned cleared his throat but his voice was husky when he spoke. 'It smells worse'n the privy behind our house. What a *stink*!'

The hob could not argue with that.

'Does it talk?'

'In a grunting sort of way, but it understands us when we speak.'

Ned jumped down from the cart and took a couple of hesitant steps towards the boggart. 'Start...putting...yer treasure...on the cobbles,' he said, raising his voice and speaking very clearly. He pointed to the ground beside the drain hole. The boggart's eyes did not flicker as it stared at Ned, and it did not move.

'Perhaps we should ask it first if it *wants* to leave the drain,' the hob said quickly. He looked at Curious. 'You do it, it likes you.'

Curious scurried over to the boggart and with much arm waving, he told it about the new lair. The boggart listened intently, then gave several deep grunts and drummed its fists on the ground. The hob watched in alarm, not sure if it was pleased or angry, but Curious did not seem in the least bit troubled by the boggart's behaviour. He turned to the hob with a wide smile. 'He likes your idea very much indeed!'

'That's good,' the hob said in relief. 'Tell it to fetch its possessions and put them on the cart. And tell it not to eat the horse.'

Curious chittered, pointed to the horse, and then pointed to the drain.

The boggart huffed and jumped down into the hole. The hob heard him splashing away along the stream.

'While the boggart's doing that, ye can show us where the box is hid,' Ned said, taking a basket of tools from the back of the cart. He looked around with a frown. 'But we need to be quick about it. Don't want to stay any longer than we have to.'

132

The hob glanced up at the south range of the abbey uneasily. Empty window frames, the glass smashed out, were dark patches against the grey stones. The wind sent dead leaves skittering across the yard and somewhere, a window shutter knocked against a wall. The kitchen door swung on rusty hinges, squealing softly.

A feeling of being watched grew steadily as they walked through the silent kitchen and out into the cloister. The walls sheltered the garden from the wind but it moaned through the rafters of the derelict ranges and set doors in empty rooms rattling and banging.

Curious led the way to the north alley, close to where his roof boss was now just blank grey stone. He peered at the wall for some moments, before bending over to look at it from upside down. 'There!' He straightened up and pointed to a patch of stones which, to the hob, looked the same as all the rest.

Ned took a hammer and chisel from his basket. He tapped the stones with the chisel blade and listened to the sound they made, and then began to chip away the mortar. 'Stand well back, both of ye.'

The hob watched as shards of stone and mortar flew from the end of Ned's chisel. Soon the first stone wobbled like a loose tooth. Ned worked it free with his fingertips and pulled it from the wall.

'There's summat in there,' he said in excitement. He loosened more stones and the hole widened steadily until he could reach inside. He dragged a wooden box out and laid it on the floor. 'Ain't very big.' He sounded disappointed.

133

The hob and Curious crouched beside him to watch as he lifted the lid. A folded linen cloth covered the contents and the hob pulled it aside.

'Books,' Ned said flatly. He sat back on his heels. 'Ain't treasure at all.'

The hob took a leather bound book from the box. 'I know this one!' He had last seen it in the house of Sir Robert of Weforde, the alchemist who tried to help banish a demon from the abbey and surrounding villages. 'This is a book of ancient magic.'

The second one belonged to Sir Robert too. Ned turned the pages and shook his head at the symbols and numbers and letters filling every last bit of parchment, then closed it and put it aside. 'More magic, I s'pose.'

There were three other books in the box. Two were large and heavy, with fine vellum pages filled with beautifully coloured drawings around the edges of the neatly written text. The last book was small, with a plain cover of worn brown leather. The hob looked inside and though he could not read the words, he saw that it had been written by several different hands. The drawings scattered through the text were simple black ink sketches. He gazed at them in astonishment. There was the angel and the feather from its wing; the crow-headed demon; the church with a hole in the roof where the tower used to be; two angels fighting; a golden acorn, and a hob. They were pictures of Crowfield's secrets.

Curious leaned over to look at the book. His mouth moved as he read the words silently.

The hob stared at him in astonishment. 'You can read?'

Curious nodded. 'I learned when the novice master taught the novices their letters.'

'What does it say?'

'It's the story of an angel who died near the abbey gates one Christmas many years ago. It was found by a man from a nearby village...'

'My mam's forefather,' Ned interrupted proudly.

'The monks buried the angel in the forest and kept the secret for a long, long time, until two strangers came to the abbey. With the help of a servant boy...'

'My friend,' the hob said with a smile, puffing out his chest.

'With his help,' Curious continued, 'they found the grave and dug up the angel but it wasn't dead. And then a demon came and pulled the bell tower down and the angel came back and fought it and killed it.'

'You have left a *lot* out of the story,' the hob said with a frown, 'such as how Sir Robert tried to use his magic to defeat the demon. These are his books and they hold very old and dark magic, but humans are not good at magic and his spells did not work against the demon. My friend, the boy Will, asked the nangel to come and help us, and it did.' He tapped the parchment sheet with a finger. 'That should all be written down.'

'It is,' Curious said, sounding flustered, 'but it is written in monk words, and I am making the words into ones you will understand and it's not very easy.'

Ned's eyes were shining and he grinned at the hobs. 'I'll learn to read and then I can use the magic in the books!'

'No,' the hob said, frowning at him sternly, 'you will *not*. Abbot Matthew was a very wise man and he knew these writings and pictures needed to be kept secret. *This* is the abbey's treasure, a treasure made of words and not gold, but worth more than all the silver and jewels a greedy man could ever own.'

Ned looked put out by this but he just shrugged. 'Ain't got time to learn to read anyhow, and ain't nobody to teach me if I did.'

'Look at this,' the hob pointed to a small, hairy creature looking out of the page at them. 'It's a hob. Which one of the brother men drew it?'

'It says...this drawing was made by Brother Mark, in the year 1348. *I have seen a creature I believe to be fay,*' Curious read slowly, following the words across the page with a fingertip. '*It stays close to Brother Snail's workshop in the abbey herb garden and does not seem to be a creature of evil intent. I shall say nothing of what I have seen. This will be a secret I share only with God and the pages of this book.*'

'That was *me!*' the hob said in a rush of excitement. 'I lived in the snail brother's hut and I remember Brother Mark.' He patted the two largest books. 'He made these.' He recalled the monk as a quiet, kindly man who spent the time, when he was not praying or sleeping, in the cloister alley, sitting at his high desk, feather quill pen in hand. He never knew the monk had been able to see him.

Curious turned the page. His eyes widened. 'This was written by Brother John.' He laid a paw gently on the parchment. The hob saw that the words were written in a bolder, heavier hand. 'He gave me my name. Every morning, he looked up at me and said that I was indeed a curious creature.' Curious read the page silently and tears gleamed in his eyes.

'Well? What else did he write?' Ned asked impatiently, prodding Curious gently in the ribs.

'Brother John found Brother Mark's drawing of the hob and when the stonemasons were mending the abbey after the demon broke it, he showed it to one of them and said it would make a fine roof boss for the cloister. The stonemason carved *me* from the drawing.'

The hob stared at Curious and a warm feeling spread through his body. In a strange way, he and Curious were family. He had never had a family of his own before and the thought sowed a seed of happiness deep inside him. 'Do the words say anything about the acorn?' he asked.

Curious turned back to the book. He pointed to a line and said, 'Here! Brother John had a dream one night of a strange creature with antlers. It came out of the forest and made its way to the cloister. Doors opened for it as if by magic. It stopped beneath the carving of the hob and held up a golden acorn. When he woke, Brother John went to the cloister alley and found that the stone hob was now holding the acorn in its paw. It had not been there the day before.'

So, the hob thought, the golden acorn was the Deerman's gift to Curious. Had he given the boggart the fay fire too?

'Does the brother man say *why* the Deerman gave the acorn to you?'

Curious shook his head. 'No, but I remember that night. It was as if I had been sleeping until the Deerman came to me. He reached up with a leafy stick and touched my paw. I felt the gleamy thing between my fingers. He told me it held old magic and would protect me. He didn't say it in words. I heard it in here,' he said, tapping his head. 'And then he went away. Brother John says that he never told anyone about his dream, and nobody ever noticed the acorn. He wrote all this down when he was very old, so that the truth would be there after he was gone.' Curious sniffed. 'I still miss him.'

'Well, ye can miss him back home in Yagleah,' Ned said as he packed the books into the box and closed the lid. 'We have to go.' He gave a sharp cry and stumbled backwards. The hob jumped in fright and turned to see what had startled the boy. No more than ten paces away, the crawling man crouched by the wall, a hunched nightmare of bones and grey rags. With a hiss like the last breath from a dying body, it gathered itself together and sprang.

Chapter Fourteen

In their panic to escape, Ned and the hobs fell over each other, legs and arms tangling together. Ned grunted with pain when he landed heavily on the box. Curious fled along the west alley, a streak of grey, trailing high-pitched wails. The hob ran to the corner of the alley, and then stopped to look back. The crawly thing held a screaming and kicking Ned by one ankle, its bone fingers gripping tightly. The hob looked around desperately for some kind of weapon, anything he could use to beat the crawling man away. All he found was a thick stub of broken branch. By now, the creature was dragging Ned towards the south door leading from the cloister to the church. The hob ran after them, his legs shaking so much they could barely hold him.

'Let go of him!' he shouted. *Was that reedy little voice really his?*

The crawling man took no notice. Ned thrashed around in terror but the thing was too strong for him. The hob hit the hunched grey back as hard as he could. The branch shattered and bits flew off, hitting the hob and Ned with sharp splinters. The hob dropped the branch and grabbed Ned's arm. He knew he was wasting his time, but he had to try. He tugged with all his strength but his feet slid on the worn tiles as the crawling thing pulled Ned along the alley floor.

What is it going to do with the boy? The hob had no doubt that whatever it was, it would be dreadful; the son of the man who had killed it would die a terrible death. The hob tugged harder, whimpering with fear. He could not let Ned die.

A hairy black shape, smelling as ripe as a midden heap, leaped onto the crawling man's back with a blood-freezing yowl. Boggart and monster tumbled and snarled and thrashed across the floor. Ned scrambled to his feet, snatched up the hob and ran. He did not stop until they reached the cart. He set the hob down and leaned against Flit, his breath harsh and ragged, his whole body shaking.

'We shouldn't've come here,' he said in a trembling, tearful voice, 'I *knew* it were askin' for trouble...'

Curious's head poked up over the side of the cart, his eyes huge and terrified. He held the golden acorn tightly in his paws. The hob saw piles of the boggart's rubbish all around him. A green glazed jar holding flames of faylight had been tucked into a corner and the wattle sides of the cart were lit with an eerie white glow. The boggart had wasted no time in loading its treasure, but where *was* the boggart? Had the crawly man killed it?

The hob looked anxiously at the kitchen door, willing the boggart to emerge. 'Don't let the crawly man harm it,' he whispered to whoever might be listening, twisting his paws together.

Ned climbed onto the seat board. 'We're leaving,' he said.

141

'No! Wait!' the hob said. 'We can't leave the boggart behind. It saved your life,' he added, seeing the indecision on the boy's face.

'If it ain't here soon, then most likely it's dead.' Ned took up the reins, but he turned to watch the kitchen door. 'First sign of that...*thing* and we're going.'

The moments crept by. Flit scraped a restless hoof on the cobbles and blew through his nostrils. *He wants to be away from the abbey as much as the rest of us,* the hob thought.

The kitchen door flew open and the boggart tumbled through. Its claws scrabbled on the cobbles and it looked around frantically. It spotted the cart and loped towards it. Ned flicked the reins and Flit lunged forward, jerking the cart into motion. The boggart jumped up on the back and turned quickly to stare at the south range. The crawling man appeared in the kitchen doorway. Moving unsteadily, it dragged itself out into the yard. It gave a high, wild howl of fury. Curious grabbed the hob in fright and the boggart huffed and thumped a fist against the side of the cart. Its eyes burned with hatred and it bared sharply pointed teeth in a snarl.

'Hup, Flit! Hup! Fast as ye can, boy!' Bracing his feet against the foot board, Ned crouched low and slapped the reins on Flit's back. The horse needed no encouragement; taking the bridge at breakneck speed and charging along the causeway, he left the crawling man far behind. The cart bounced and swayed and the hob was terrified it was going to overturn. He clung to the side and Curious clung to him. The

142

boggart seemed more concerned about its treasure and threw itself across the piles of cloths and baskets to stop them falling off the back of the cart. Ned did not allow Flit to slow down until they reached the ford across the Sheep Brook.

'Is it still after us?' the boy called breathlessly over his shoulder as he guided Flit down into the shallow stream.

'No,' the hob said, staring back along the empty track.

'That was too close by half.'

'You didn't close the gate,' Curious said, his voice a worried whimper. 'What if it gets out of the abbey and follows us?'

'I don't think it *can* leave,' the hob said. The abbey seemed to have a way of holding spirits inside its walls. He knew Urchin and Mary Magdalene would have left long ago if they could have.

Now that its belongings were no longer in danger, the boggart settled itself with its back against the side of the cart. The hob saw the dark gleam of blood on its chest fur. It touched the wound with a claw and grunted softly. The hob heard pain in the sound and felt a rush of pity.

'Oh no!' Ned said, putting a hand on his head. 'We left the box behind!'

The hob stared at him in dismay. After all that, they had left the abbey's precious secrets on the cloister floor for anyone to find. Nobody suggested going back for it.

The journey continued in silence. The hob sat in a miserable huddle in a corner of the cart. They had let the brother men down. All the long years they had kept their silence about the nangel and the other strange happenings at Crowfield Abbey, and now it was all for nothing.

Perhaps, the hob thought wretchedly, *if we find Urchin's father and take him to the abbey, we can go back for the box.* But then he thought of the crawly man and unhappiness settled heavily on his shoulders. It would never let them do that. They had escaped with their lives this time. They would not be so lucky again.

***

By late morning, the last of the boggart's treasure had been carried from the cart and piled up outside the burial mound. The passages and chambers were too narrow and low for the boggart but he told Curious that he could easily make them bigger. When it was time to say goodbye and leave, the hob found the boggart already hard at work, clawing at the roof of the entrance passage and piling earth into a basket to take outside. Small bowls of faylight stood by the entrance and the smell was terrible. The creature seemed quite at home.

'Humf hnurf.' The boggart reached out a muddy hand and gathered the hob into an evil-smelling, hairy embrace. 'Fnarf.'

'You're welcome,' the hob said breathlessly. He scurried back outside as soon as the boggart dropped him on the ground and gasped in great lungfuls of fresh air. Curious said his goodbyes and returned to the cart with mud on his tunic and tears in his eyes.

'We can come and visit whenever you want,' the hob assured him. 'I think the boggart would like that.'

Ned stood by the mound and shook his head slowly. 'If ye didn't know there was a way in, ye'd never guess from lookin' at it.'

'Fay magic,' the hob said. 'The old elf hid it from prying eyes and the magic must still be working.'

The hob looked up at the sky and saw that the clouds had cleared. The wind had worn itself out. Stillness lay over the forest and fields and there was a chill in the air. He thought about the Cold Fair and wished he did not have to go there. But a promise was a promise.

They reached the village and saw a crowd of people on the green outside Ned's home. Some were on horseback, some on foot.

'It's Sir Samuel, talking to my father,' Ned said. He sounded worried. 'That ain't good. The steward's with him, and so is her ladyship, his sour-faced wife.'

The hob and Curious crouched down on the foot board, hidden from sight by Flit's rump. The people with Sir Samuel, men and women in brightly coloured clothes, blocked the lane to the carpenter's house with their horses. Unable to pass, Ned stopped the cart at the side of the road.

'...clumsy oaf! You have only your own stupidity to blame,' Sir Samuel shrilled.

The hob saw the angry colour flood Ned's cheeks. The boy's hands gripped the reins tightly and his body shook. 'He can't talk to my father like that!'

The hob poked Ned in the back. 'Stay quiet, or he will be angry with you too.'

Noll Swyfte stood a little way apart from the rest of his family and the villagers who had gathered to watch. His face was a white mask of fury as he stared up at the lord of the manor.

'I knew it was a mistake to hire you,' Sir Samuel went on, his voice rising and his jowls wobbling. 'You are a work-shy wastrel, Swyfte. How many of my carved stones have you broken? Eh? Well?'

'I brought ye all the ones we found,' Noll said. His fists clenched and unclenched at his sides and his eyes narrowed dangerously.

'And a liar too!' Sir Samuel looked around at his companions with a triumphant smile, as if he had just proved some great truth. There were smirks and a ripple of laughter. 'You see what these country people are like? Do you see *now* what I have to put up with?'

Beside him, a thin, sharp-faced woman on a white mare nodded in agreement. Her large teeth protruded over her lower lip and she had a spiteful look about her. She was dressed in an unflattering shade of red that made her skin look sallow. The hob did not like her.

'I cannot bear to look at these...*creatures* a moment longer,' she said peevishly, lifting a dried orange studded with cloves to her nose and sniffing delicately. 'It's enough that we have to live in this godforsaken place, amidst such squalor and uncleanliness, without having to be this close to these common labourers. God alone knows what we might catch from them. We should go home to London, husband...'

'Yes, yes, my dear,' Sir Samuel said impatiently. From his expression, the hob guessed he had heard all this many times before.

'That's Lady Ryce,' Ned whispered, 'Sir Samuel's wife. She ain't nice.'

Sir Samuel straightened his shoulders and puffed out his chest and looked for all the world, the hob decided, like an ill-tempered pigeon. He waved a hand at the houses around the green and the small wood between his land and the village. 'When I cut down those trees, I will be forced to look at these hovels.' He turned to his steward, sitting silent and still on his brown mare. 'That will not do, Master Dunch. These wretched little houses will have to be removed, starting with Swyfte's place.'

Shocked gasps swept through the villagers on the green.

'Ye can't cut down the coppice!' a woman called. 'Them's *our* trees!'

Noll stared at the woman for a moment, brows raised. 'His lordship's talking about pulling down our houses, ye daft woman,' he snapped. 'Cuttin' down a few trees is the least of our worries.'

Angry mutters went around the crowd of villagers, but nobody, it seemed, was brave enough to speak up.

Sir Samuel's jowls quivered more violently. 'How *dare* you speak to me like that in my own village! I'll have every building in Yagleah taken down!'

Master Dunch's lips drew into a thin line. Anger darkened his eyes but whether it was with the lord of the manor or the villagers, the hob could not guess. He remained silent and stared straight ahead, but Sir Samuel did not seem to notice.

'Yes, pull them all down!' Lady Ryce said in a voice as flinty as her eyes. 'Every last filthy little pigsty.'

'I will increase your rent, Swyfte, and it'll teach you not to cross me,' Sir Samuel said, glaring at Noll.

'Ain't going to get much rent if ye knock his house down,' someone called.

Sir Samuel looked as if he was about to choke with fury. His scarlet cheeks wobbled like frogspawn and his eyes bulged.

Master Dunch leaned forward in his saddle and said, 'You can't raise Swyfte's rent, my lord.'

'I most certainly can!' Sir Samuel blustered.

'No,' Master Dunch said evenly, 'Swyfte is a tenant of Goodman Cooper at Bethlehem Farm. He does not pay rent to you.'

This seemed to enrage Sir Samuel still further. 'Then I will speak to Goodman Cooper and have this good-for-nothing labourer turned out of his house!'

'Ye nasty, evil old...' Ned murmured. The hob prodded him in the back again. If Sir Samuel heard him, it would just bring more trouble down on his family.

The church bell clanged out, calling the villagers and the people from the manor to worship. A little of the tension on the green subsided. Sir Samuel and his wife glared at Noll before turning their horses' heads and riding off along the road. Their friends followed, but Master Dunch remained where he was. He watched his companions until they were riding up the hill towards the church before turning to Noll.

'I will see that you are paid what you are owed, Swyfte. And as for pulling the village down, that will not happen.' He hesitated for a couple of moments, as if trying to decide whether or not to say more. 'I believe...Sir Samuel and Lady Ryce are thinking of returning to their London house. Country life does not, eh, suit them.'

Noll stared at him through narrowed eyes. 'What about his lordship's fine new house?' The contempt in his voice was clear. 'And the view from his windows?'

Master Dunch did not reply at first. Perhaps he did not feel comfortable discussing his master's affairs with a village labourer, the hob thought.

'I am not sure that the new house will ever be finished,' the steward said, 'so Sir Samuel might not be in need of a view after all. We will see. Kit Barefote told me how you came to fall from the scaffolding.'

Noll looked away.

'I did not tell Sir Samuel the full story, just that there was an accident and you were injured, as he could see for himself today.'

'Much *he* cares!' Noll muttered. 'And Tobias, he was hurt an' all. He ain't going to be working again this side of Christmas.'

'No, I don't suppose he will,' Master Dunch said. 'I'm sorry.' With that, he turned his mare and rode across the green. He did not seem to be in a hurry to catch up with his master.

'What 'bout our coppice?' someone called after him but the steward gave no sign that he heard.

'Well, if he ain't finishing his new build, he ain't going to cut down the coppice, is he?' Noll said.

The tolling bell called the villagers away from the green. People had washed their faces and hands and they wore their best clothes, which in most cases were their everyday clothes with the worst of the stains and mud scrubbed off. The hob watched as they walked away up the hill.

'See to Flit and hurry after us,' Agnes called as she followed her neighbours. Noll limped slowly along behind his family, silent and deep in thought.

Ned jiggled the reins and Flit trotted towards the carpenter's house. The hob climbed up onto the seat board beside the boy.

'Ye can settle yerselves by the fire till we come back,' Ned said, smiling down at him. 'Later, we'll go and see Bess and ask her about the Cold Fair. Ain't much she don't know about ghosts and magic and the like.'

The hob nodded. He would be glad of a chance to warm himself and rest for a while. He looked up at Ned's scratched and bruised face and felt a surge of remorse. The boy had come close to death that day. It was not right or fair to expect him to go looking for the ghostly fair but he was not sure if he was brave enough to go by himself.

'I hid some bread and a bowl of milk for ye by the cupboard,' Ned went on. 'Should still be there unless the cat's had it. He ain't supposed to be in the house but he gets in somehow, and he ain't one ye want to cross! Nasty, he is, but a good ratter.'

The hob laid a paw on Ned's knee. 'Thank you.'

'It's only a bit of old bread,' Ned said with a grin.

'You are a brave, true friend,' the hob said. '*That* is what I am thanking you for.'

Ned's cheeks reddened but he looked pleased. 'Ye're right welcome. And I wish ye luck with the cat.'

Chapter Fifteen

The hob heard the family return from church long before he saw them. The children shouted and squabbled, and Mam shouted even louder to try and quieten them. He waited anxiously for Ned to come and take them to see Bess but the boy was kept busy with chores. He saw the daylight beyond the window fade as the family gathered at the table to eat. The smell of pottage was appetising and the hob hoped there would be a little left for him and Curious. He had not eaten warm pottage since he had lived at the abbey two hundred years ago. He had long since forgotten what it tasted like but the smell began to stir old memories.

When the meal was finished and the table cleared, Ned poked his head around the corner of the cupboard.

'Are ye ready?' he whispered.

The hob hid his disappointment at the lack of pottage and nodded.

'Meet me outside in the yard.' With that, Ned was gone.

The family were quieter now, sitting around the fire while Mam told them a story, the baby asleep in a basket by her feet. Noll dozed in his chair. The hob took the painted sky from its hiding place. He did not want to leave it behind, just in case someone found it and decided it would make good kindling for the fire. Curious brought his acorn and nobody noticed them slip out of the house.

Ned was waiting by the gate, rubbing his arms against the cold. His breath clouded around his head. 'Follow me,' he said.

They left the yard and crossed the green in the frosty dusk. There was nobody about but smoke rose from chimneys or holes in thatch like threads of grey wool. The hob sniffed the air. The smell of cooking food made his stomach growl hungrily. It seemed like most of Yagleah was sitting down to a meal of pottage that day.

To one side of the coppice, a small thatched house of timber and lime-washed plaster stood inside a blackthorn hedge. Ned pushed open the gate and nodded for the hobs to go inside. A gravel path led between vegetable and herb beds, past a huge old apple tree, to the door. It opened before they reached it and Bess stood there, a small dark shape against the lantern light behind her.

'In ye come,' she said, standing aside.

The hob gazed around the house. There was just one room, with a loft over one end. It was warm and clean and furnished simply, with just a table, bench, two chests and chair. Shelves around the walls held pots and bowls, jars and small boxes. Bundles of dried herbs hung from hooks beneath the shelves while baskets hung from the beams beneath the loft. A lantern stood on the table in a pool of yellow light. There was a stone hearth in the middle of the floor and an iron pot stood over the fire on a trivet. The smells coming from it were even more appetising than the ones in Ned's house.

Curious sat by the fire and laid his golden acorn on the floor beside him.

Bess nodded to the hob's painted panel. 'What's that ye got there?'

The hob held it up. The stars gleamed softly in the lantern light.

'That's right beautiful,' Bess said, smiling. 'A rare treasure indeed.'

'It came from the abbey church,' the hob said.

The woman sighed and shook her head, a look of sadness in her blue eyes. 'Shame to see such a fine old building brought to ruin.'

The hob nodded. He stood uncertainly in the middle of the floor, clutching the panel.

'We're here to ask ye about the Cold Fair,' Ned said. 'Brother Walter has business there.'

Bess raised her eyebrows at the hob's strange name. 'Is that so?' she said. 'Well, it's a cold old night and maybe ye'd like somethin' to eat before goin' out again. Sit yerselves by the fire.' She glanced at Curious in his woollen tunic and her gaze softened. 'Are ye hungry, little man?'

Curious nodded. 'Oh yes, indeed!'

Her mouth twitching into a smile, Bess filled three wooden bowls with barley and vegetable pottage and handed them to Ned and the hobs. Ned forgot to mention that he had already eaten, the hob noticed, but then he thought that Bess probably knew that and didn't mind.

Ned pulled up the stool to the fireside to eat his meal. The hob sat on the floor beside him, sipping the pottage from the bowl and picking out the pieces of leek and turnip with his fingers. Curious managed to spill more food down the front of his tunic than he ate. Ned nudged Curious with his foot. 'I'll have to teach ye to use a spoon. It'll save ye wearin' yer food 'stead of eatin' it.'

Bess settled herself in the chair by the fire. She looked at Ned and frowned. 'Where did ye get those bruises and scratches, boy? Ye didn't have them last time I saw ye.'

Ned told her about his fight with the crawling man. She stared at him in horror.

'Ye went *back* to the abbey? After what happened to yer father and Kit? Ned, are ye daft, boy? If Noll found out, he'd be hopping on one foot with anger. Ye could have been hurt, or *killed*!'

'Well, I wasn't,' Ned said stubbornly, but the hob saw that he was upset.

'Don't ye *ever* go near that abbey again, do ye hear me? Not Ever.'

'I won't,' Ned said.

Bess frowned at him for a few moments then sighed. She turned her attention to the hob.

'So why are ye goin' lookin' for the Cold Fair?' she said. 'Why would ye want to do that?'

The hob explained about Urchin and her father. 'She can't leave the abbey without him,' he finished, 'so I promised to bring him to her.'

'That was a very big promise to make,' Bess said. 'What do ye know 'bout the fair?'

'I told him about the sweating sickness and the fair being moved to Lammas. I told him it's a ghost fair now,' Ned said, wiping his mouth on the back of his hand. His bowl was licked clean.

Bess nodded slowly. 'That's all true, but there's more to the tale than that. Did ye know the fair was cursed by a wise woman from Weforde?'

'No,' Ned said in surprise. 'Ain't never heard about that before.'

'The last year of the fair, it was a bitter cold October. Frost had set hard a week before and the river were frozen enough to skate on, but people still brought their sheep to the fair. Chapmen and traders came along too, and with them came the sweating sickness. It spread like wildfire and many people died. The wise woman, Sweet Cecily, came to the Cold Fair with her two daughters, to sell possets and potions and jars of honey. Well, the family all sickened and only Sweet Cecily survived. She couldn't bury her children for weeks, not until a thaw set in at All Hallows. Some say she went mad with grief.

She cursed the fair and all those who were there that year. Many of them were already dead and she doomed their souls to return to the fair field for those three days every year, for evermore. The dead cannot leave the fair and if any living soul is foolish enough to go near it, they'll be dragged in and never be seen alive again.'

The only sound in the room was the crackle of the fire. A log shifted and sparks snapped and danced briefly on the hearthstones. One landed on Curious's tail and he squeaked in alarm as he patted it out with a paw.

The hob saw the shadow of fear in Ned's eyes. 'That's why Father and Mam always tell us not to go near the fair field at this time o' the year,' Ned said softly.

Bess nodded. 'Jack Thatcher went up there when he was a boy and he swore afterwards he saw the ghosts. It frightened what few wits he had right out of his head, but even he had enough sense not to go too near.'

Bess turned to the hob. 'I think ye'd be wise to forget about the ghost girl and her father. Ye can't help them.'

The hob thought she was probably right but the thought of Urchin was like a thorn in his paw. He sat in unhappy silence and gazed into the fire. He wished with all his might that he had not made his promise to her. *I gave her hope and now I am going to break her heart,* he thought. *I am not a good friend.*

'Have *ye* ever seen the fair?' Ned asked.

'No, but I heard it twice, both times at dusk. I heard music and people shoutin' and talkin', and sheep bleating, but I didn't see a thing,' Bess said. 'People say the fair is only there at dusk or dawn, when the door between the Otherworld and this one opens just a crack.' She smiled at the hob. 'Ye should know that, being a fay creature.'

The hob just shrugged. For him the door was always open. Perhaps Sweet Cecily's curse was only strong enough to make it appear at the threshold times, when all magic was at its most potent.

'The woman sounds very bad,' Curious said.

Bess sighed. 'I don't know if she was or she wasn't. Cecily came from a long line of wise women, as far back as Dame Alys of Weforde. Now *she* was evil and her magic was strong. She had a white crow and she released a demon from beneath the floor of the abbey church, they do say. Her blood ran strong in Sweet Cecily's veins, so who knows?'

'But not all wise women are evil, are they?' Ned said softly, smiling at Bess.

She smiled back. 'Bless you, boy, no! Of course not.'

The hob said nothing. He remembered Dame Alys only too well. Her magic had let the demon loose from the spell that held it prisoner beneath the church floor, but she was as frightened as everyone else when it began to destroy the abbey and villages nearby,

159

and kill people. She believed the demon was an ancient god of her ancestors, but she was wrong; it was an angel of darkness and death.

The hob shifted restlessly and pushed those memories from his mind. 'Does the woman's magic stop hobs from going to the fair?'

'Well, I don't rightly know,' Bess said slowly, as she considered this. 'Ye still thinking of going up to the fair field, are ye?'

The hob nodded. Urchin had saved him from the crawling man, even though she must have been terrified of it. He could not let his fear turn him aside from helping her.

'It's too dangerous,' Ned said anxiously. 'Ye might get trapped in the fair and never come back.'

'Perhaps Sweet Cicely's magic only traps humans,' the hob said, 'and sheep. Perhaps she did not have strong enough magic to curse a fay.'

Bess regarded him thoughtfully for a while. 'Indeed, why would she curse fays at all? The Good Folk didn't bring the sweating sickness. Ye might be safe enough from her curse, right enough. But there ain't no point in going there now. It's long past dusk. Ye'll have to wait until dawn.' She left her chair, took a basket down from a shelf and set it on the table to rummage through it. 'I have somethin' here which might keep ye safe. It's been passed down in my family for many years. My forefather found it in the snow one day when...' she hesitated, but the hob knew what she was going to say.

'When he found the nangel.'

160

'Ye know about that?' She smiled and shook her head. 'Ye seem to know a lot about what's happened around here over the years.'

'Brother Walter was living at the abbey when the angel's grave was dug up,' Ned interrupted, his face flushing with excitement. Bess looked at the hob in astonishment.

'And Bess, it wasn't dead!'

'Is that so? I think ye need to tell me the whole story.'

With frequent interruptions from Ned, the hob told her about how the Dark King of the Unseelie Court had shot the angel and how it had been dug from its grave a hundred years later, none the worse for a century spent under the earth.

Bess listened, her face pale, her eyes shining. When the hob finished his story, she took a folded scrap of faded linen from the basket. Inside it lay a small white feather, no longer than the hob's finger. There was something about the feather's pale glow that told him it was from the angel's wing.

'The monks had another feather,' the hob said, 'but it was much bigger than this one.'

'My forefather hid this feather away and never told the monks what he'd found. They'd have taken it from him if they'd known.' She held it out to him. 'There's a power here I ain't never felt from anything else before. It'll protect ye, and might help ye take the

161

chapman's ghost from the fair. Ye'll need strong magic to do that, but an angel's power is stronger than Sweet Cicely's curse.'

The hob took the feather from Bess. It weighed nothing but made his fingers tingle as he stroked it gently. He wrapped it carefully in the linen.

'Wait, ye'll need something to hold it safe,' Bess said, taking another basket from the shelf. She took out a small leather purse with a cord strap and put it over his head. She tucked the wad of linen inside. The purse hung down to the hob's knees, so she tied a knot in the cord to shorten it.

'There. That'll do right well.'

'How will I find the fair field?' the hob asked.

'I told ye I'd show ye the way,' Ned said.

'Ye must not go anywhere near the fair!' Bess said sharply.

'I'll just take him to the end of the track.'

'See ye don't go a step further, then, just as far as Sir Samuel's new fence around our common.'

'I won't.'

Bess gazed at him uncertainly. She did not look happy. 'Maybe I should come with ye.'

A look of relief lit Ned's face. 'Ye don't have to,' he said but the hob could tell he wanted Bess to come with them very badly indeed.

'Very well. Be here shortly before first light and we'll go together. The moon is close to full so it'll light the way.' She leaned forward in her chair and pointed to Curious's acorn. 'What's that ye got, little hob?'

Curious held it out to her and watched as she examined it.

'This is a rare treasure, and magic too. Where did ye find it?'

'The Deerman gave it to me when I was a stone hob.'

'Who is the Deerman?' Bess asked uneasily.

'He's the one who brought the stones and the wall paintings in the abbey to life. He takes them away to the forest,' the hob said.

'That's why Noll could never find any carvings.' Bess said softly. 'I never knew there was so much old magic still out there. Is the Deerman a fay?'

'I don't know what he is,' the hob said.

Bess said nothing for a while. 'I think I would like to see him for myself,' she said.

'I don't think he concerns himself with humans,' the hob said. He saw the disappointment in Bess's face and added quickly, 'But you *might* see him one day, perhaps.'

She nodded. 'I hope so.'

'Best be off home. It's getting late and Mam will be wondering where I've got to,' Ned said, getting to his feet.

The hob held up his panel of painted sky. 'Can I leave this here?'

163

'I'll keep it safe for ye,' Bess said, taking it from him and putting it on a shelf.

Ned grinned. 'It'll be safer here than in my house. Mam'll probably put it on the fire.'

The hob nodded. 'That is what I thought.' He was relieved that Ned had not taken offence. He did not want the boy to think he was ungrateful for the kindly offer of a home but the truth was he was too set in his ways to be happy in such a bustling, noisy household. He did not want to live in a place where he had to hide his painted sky. He was beginning to think he would have to tell Ned that he and Curious were going to find somewhere else, somewhere more peaceful, to live.

Bess walked to the door with the boy and the hobs. 'I will wait for ye by the gate shortly before dawn, when the first birds start to sing.'

'We'll be there,' Ned said. Bess watched from her gate as they hurried across the green, the grass crisp with ice beneath their feet. The moon had not yet risen and the houses alongside the green were just black shapes against the starry sky. The hob laid a paw over the purse around his neck and felt courage seep through his bones, as comforting as warm honey. He knew he was going to need it before the night was over.

Chapter Sixteen

The rest of the household was sound asleep when the hob and Curious left their corner beside the cupboard and went to wait for Ned by the back door in the cross passage. The sound of Noll's snores rumbled from the parlour. Ned crept down from the loft to meet them and drew back the bolts to open the door. A draught of freezing air swept into the house and Ned quickly ushered the hobs outside. He closed the door quietly behind them.

The hob ran along the path at the back of the house and turned the corner into the yard. Curious kept close to him, with Ned a couple of paces behind. The moonlight was bright and it turned the yard to a maze of glimmering frost and shadows. They ran past the carpentry sheds and out onto the green.

Curious lagged a little way behind. Ned went back for him and lifted him onto his shoulders.

A shadow moved out from the hedge by Bess's gate. The wise woman was wrapped in a dark cloak and her face, peering out from beneath her hood, was as white as the moon.

They hurried up the sloping village street towards the church. The street curved around the graveyard and headed off into the moonlit distance between fields and woodland. In the east, dawn drew a faint line of light along the horizon. If the fair was going to appear, it would do so now.

They reached the turning to the old drove road just beyond the last village house. Between the high banks and hedges, the way ahead was lost in darkness. They kept to the grass along the edge to avoid twisting an ankle in an unseen rut.

'Listen!' the hob said. Somewhere up ahead, someone was playing a flute, the notes as sharp as pins in the frozen stillness.

'It's there,' Bess whispered, 'the fair!'

They reached the gate to a huge sheep pasture. The drove road continued beyond it and the banks on either side, stripped of their hedges, were dark lines on the flank of the hill. Ned lifted Curious from his shoulders and sat him on the top bar of the gate.

Bess peered ahead, turning her head to listen to the whispers of sounds that were growing behind the notes of the flute. The hob peered between the bars of the gate but there was nothing to see, just the sweep of pasture beneath the moon, and the sheep.

'Should we go a bit further?' Ned asked.

'We'll go a little way. Ye stop when I tell ye, though.'

Curious jumped down from the gate, while the hob squeezed through the gap between two bars. Ned helped Bess over, and then climbed after her. Keeping close to the bank, they made their way towards the fair field. It was surrounded by a shallow ditch, roughly square in shape. Wisps of white mist trailed across the frosty ground inside the ditch and the hob saw them slowly form into pale figures.

'Look!' Curious breathed. 'All the white people!'

166

Bess held up her hand. 'Ssh! Quiet, now.'

The figures moved silently between misty shapes which gradually turned into booths and stalls. There were carts and packhorses, and campfires and braziers burning cold and white. It was a fair of darkness and light, with the colour washed away. The hob felt a deep reluctance to go any closer. He wanted nothing more than to run away as fast as his legs would allow and leave the ghosts to their fair, then he thought of Urchin and knew he had no choice but to finish this.

They crouched low and kept to the shelter of the bank. Bess led the way and she stopped every few steps to listen and watch. The hob stayed close behind her.

The people did not look quite right, the hob thought uneasily. It was as if their ghosts had not fully remembered what their living bodies had looked like: gaunt faces and hollow eyes, clothes that looked as if they had been buried in the earth for years. An air of decay hung over everything, from the tattered cloths covering the booths and stalls to the skeletally thin horses and dogs. Even the fires in the iron braziers and in pits in the ground looked as if the heat had left them long ago and only the pale memories of the flames remained.

The drove road skirted the southern side of the fair field. The bank had been worn away in places, as if people had used gaps in a long vanished hedge to reach the fair. Bess, Ned and the hobs knelt behind a low hump of bank and peered over the top. The clamour of

167

singing, talking and traders crying their wares could be heard but it sounded faint and far away. Curious whispered, 'I don't like this.'

'Nor me,' Ned said softly.

The hob gazed at the fair in dismay. Urchin had described her father in colours – his patched coat of blue, green and gold. *How will I find him, when everything is grey?*

'Are ye sure ye still want to do this?' Bess whispered nervously.

The hob nodded but his stomach was tying itself into knots of terror.

'Then keep the feather close, and don't ye stay a moment longer than ye need to.'

'Take care, Brother Walter,' Ned said softly.

Mustering all his courage, the hob left the shelter of the bank and crossed the ditch. His legs were shaking as he edged his way into the ghostly crowd. The sounds grew louder and now he could hear the rusty whine of a hurdy gurdy keeping time with a flute and a drum. Nearby, a dog barked. Cattle lowed and geese honked, and quacking came from a basket of ducks. He passed a pen of sickly looking sheep. Their wool was matted with dirt and trailed in draggled hanks from their thin bodies. They stood motionless, their bony faces as white as skulls, their eyes dark with death. Anger pushed up through his fear. *How could Sweet Cicely have done this to so many creatures who had done her no harm?*

168

The hob jumped with fright when a skinny old woman with straggly hair and no teeth stopped in front of him. She crouched down, so that her face was close to his. Colourless eyes peered at him narrowly and a bony hand poked out from beneath a grey shawl and reached towards him. He watched her warily, ready to run if he had to.

'Tell yer fortune, pretty one?' the old woman wheedled.

The hob backed away from her. Nobody had ever called him *pretty* before, and he was not sure he liked it now.

The woman sniffed the air and her withered face puckered into a grimace. '*Blood stink*! Ye ain't like us, pretty.' Quick as light, her hand grabbed for him but her fingers went straight through his body. The hob felt as if he had been doused with icy water and gasped in shock. He turned and fled through the crowd in panic. He reached a row of booths and stalls and stopped to see if the woman was chasing him but she was nowhere to be seen.

Something large loomed over him. He saw large paws and the glint of sharp teeth behind a leather muzzle. The creature was a bear, up on its hind legs. It wore a halter, at the other end of which was a scarecrow man with no hair and a face pocked and pitted like a puddle in the rain. The man swung a stick and hit the bear across the rump. 'Dance,' he growled.

The bear did a slow turn, its eyes full of dull misery and the last trace of defiance.

'Nasty man,' the hob said, his voice trembling with fury, 'to do that to an animal. Bears do *not* dance!'

The man sneered at the hob and yanked the halter viciously. The bear stumbled and waved its front paws helplessly. Prodding the bear with the stick, the man and the animal disappeared into the crowd.

The hob felt sick with pity. How terrible to spend your life being beaten and made to dance for humans, when all you wanted was to be in the forest with your own kind; but how much worse to be forced to do it after your death, when your spirit should be free.

Anxiety gnawed at the hob and he knew he had to get away from the fair. The dead air and a creeping feeling of hopelessness weighed like lead on his body. He had the terrible feeling that if he did not leave this place soon, he might *never* be able to escape. The wise woman's curse was strong and he could feel it wrap itself around him, trapping him like a fly in a spider's web. He would not be able to fight against it for much longer, he realised fearfully. His paw shook as he held the feather in its leather purse tightly and he felt sure that it was only the feather's protection that had kept him safe this long. He had to find Jack Gaudy and get away from the fair *now*.

The crowd parted and the hob saw a scrawny little man dressed in a patchwork coat, leaning on a stick and staring into the distance. A strange looking leather bag with two wooden pipes hung from a strap over his back and the hob guessed that this must be a bagpipe. The man's face, just bone beneath lined grey skin, held no expression. A cloth spread on the grass in front of him was covered in an assortment of small trinkets, bundles of ribbons, little pieces of lace, brooches and pins. *He must be Urchin's father!* the hob thought in relief. He hurried over to the chapman but the dead eyes did not even flicker in his direction.

'Urchin is waiting for you at the abbey.' The hob had to shout to be heard above the noise around them.

Slowly the chapman's eyes moved. He gazed down at the hob and there was the merest glimmer of awareness in their grey depths.

'She is waiting for you to come for her.'

The thin lips parted and a dry, rasping voice that sounded as if it was being torn up from the roots of the earth said, 'Urchin? *My* Urchin?'

The hob nodded eagerly. 'Yes, yes! At the abbey!' He was alarmed to see people around them turning to stare.

'The... abbey?' Jack Gaudy's face twisted into a frown. 'I don't know where that is...'

'I will take you there,' the hob said, glancing in terror at the crowd of people starting to drift towards them in a silent grey tide.

Moving stiffly, the chapman knelt down and gathered up the corners of the cloth. His wares fell together in a jumble as he lifted them and he pushed the bundle into a battered old leather pack. Leaning heavily on the stick, he stood up. With a huge effort, he slung

171

the pack onto his shoulder with the bagpipe, and his body bent beneath its weight.

'This way,' the hob urged him. 'Quickly!' He turned to go but the crowd blocked his way. Jack Gaudy lifted his stick and swung it feebly at them. 'Ge' away! Move, all o' ye, now!'

Sullenly, the people shuffled aside. His fur bristling in panic, the hob ran past them and jumped across the ditch. He looked to see if Jack Gaudy was following him.

The chapman shuffled to the edge of the ditch and stopped. He shook his head. 'I can't leave the fair. 'T'won't let me.'

'Try again,' the hob called desperately. 'Try harder!'

Jack Gaudy's face crumpled with the effort of forcing a foot across the ditch. He closed his eyes and gasped but did not move. 'Can't.'

'Urchin *needs* you,' the hob said.

'I'm *tryin'*,' the man said, his voice rough with anguish. He seemed to gather himself. His body shook as he lifted a foot and pushed himself forward with his stick. The toe of his boot hung over the dip of the ditch. His lips drew back, showing discoloured stumps of teeth, and he groaned as if in pain. A low rumbling growl rose behind him. The grey crowd surged forward, arms outstretched, fingers bent to claws, as if to haul the chapman back.

What can I do? the hob thought. The paw clutching the feather grew warm and he stared down at it in astonishment. Without stopping to think, he jumped the ditch again and stood beside the chapman. The crowd was only a few paces away now and, hoping he was not doing something foolish, he stepped into Jack Gaudy's ghostly grey form. A bitter chill stopped his breath for a shocked moment. A shudder went through the freezing air around him. As one, he and the chapman tumbled forward in a sudden rush, into the ditch and up the other side. The hob fell to his knees, feeling as if his blood had turned to ice. His whole body hurt. The chapman staggered a couple of paces further before slumping to the ground and lying there.

The hob stared at him in fright. Would the curse destroy Jack Gaudy now that he had escaped from the field? What if he disappeared, to go wherever it was that human spirits were supposed to go? What would happen to Urchin then?

Ned, Curious and Bess rushed over to crouch beside the hob. Anxious hands and paws helped him to his feet.

'Ye all right, little hob?' Bess asked.

The hob managed to nod. 'I...I think so.'

'Look,' Ned breathed, pointing to the fair. People had gathered along the edge of the ditch, their faces warped into nightmarish masks of fury. The music and singing had stopped. A howl broke from countless dead throats. *'Come back, come back!'*

Other voices took up the chant and the sound rose above the field, a wild noise full of pain and rage. Ned, wide eyed with terror, grabbed Curious and lifted him onto his shoulders, and then fled back

173

along the drove road. Bess, her face stark white, hesitated for just a moment before running after them.

The hob crouched beside Jack Gaudy, his paws holding tightly to the feather. 'Do not listen to them,' he urged. 'Don't go back there.'

The shrieks and howls were no longer words. A quick glimpse at the twisted faces and snatching fingers made the hob hope very much indeed that they could not cross the ditch.

The chapman sat up, struggling under the burden of his pack. Using his stick, he slowly hauled himself to his feet. He turned his back on the fair and moved away, drifting across the grass like thistledown. The hob ran ahead of him. By the time they reached the gate, the hob was astonished to see that the man's back was a little straighter. His face seemed to have changed too. He did not look quite so frail and old.

Ned, Curious and Bess stood a little way along the road. They seemed to be listening to something up ahead.

'Hide!' Bess called urgently. She disappeared into the darkness beneath the hedge. Lifting Curious from his shoulders and holding him in his arms, Ned dived for cover nearby. The hob ran to the gate and climbed between the bars, then crouched in the hedgerow. He watched Jack Gaudy walk through the gate as if it was not there and fade into the lattice of moonlight and shadows amongst the overhanging branches.

The sound of hoof beats and an angry voice reached the hob. He recognised the querulous tones of Sir Samuel. 'I will have them pilloried and whipped for this! Waking my household with their revelry, and trespassing on my land!'

'Ain't yer land,' Ned said softly from the darkness.

'But Sir Samuel, the stories about this place...' Master Dunch said apprehensively.

'If I hear one more word from you about *ghosts*,' Sir Samuel's voice shook with fury, 'I will have you whipped too. You've let these villagers get away with too much, Master Dunch. It ends tonight, one way or another. *I* am the lord of Yagleah Manor and I will *not* take such insolence from these...these *peasants*.'

A line of horsemen rode past the hob's hiding place. None of them noticed Jack Gaudy's pale wraith. Sir Samuel turned in his saddle and pointed to one of the men riding behind him. 'You! Open the gate.'

The frenzied cries coming from the fair field were loud than ever as the ghosts raged against Sweet Cicely's curse.

'The impudence!' Sir Samuel shouted. 'I will have every last one of them up before the manor court! Hurry, man! Get that gate open *now*!'

When the last of the horses was out of sight around the bend in the road, Ned shuffled over to the hob. His teeth gleamed in the moonlight and the hob realised the boy was grinning.

'Any moment now...' Ned whispered gleefully.

A confusion of shouts and yells and the whinnies of panicked horses drowned out the noise of the fair. Hooves thundered on the drove road. Terror-stricken horses and wild-eyed riders streaked through the open gate and back along the road. Sir Samuel was a short way behind the others, his mouth open in a soundless scream as he clung to his horse's neck.

'I think,' Ned said when the riders had disappeared, 'Sir Samuel might believe in ghosts *now*.'

Bess, Ned and the hobs made their way back to the village with Jack Gaudy trailing behind like a drift of mist. The hob could still hear the yowls and screeches faintly as they walked along the road past the church. *They must be disturbing many a sleep tonight,* the hob thought, *and if Sir Samuel ever sleeps again, it will be a wonder.*

In the early dawn light, Bess's face was drawn with worry. She eyed the chapman warily and then glanced at Ned. 'Folk'll be up and about soon, if they ain't already with all this clamour goin' on. We can't risk anyone seein' us in the company of a ghost and two fays. They'll most likely burn us both for witches, boy.'

Ned looked alarmed by this. 'Would they really do that?'

'I don't want to find out,' Bess said.

The hob stared around anxiously. Light was already showing in the windows of several houses. Even though few people could see hobs, there was a fair chance most people would see Jack Gaudy. The hob knew Bess was right to be worried; it was a risk they could not take.

'I will take the chapman to the abbey *now*,' the hob said. For all he knew, Jack Gaudy's ghost would disappear with the dawn and the chance to bring father and daughter together would vanish with him. He saw that Curious was heavy-eyed with exhaustion and in spite of the woollen tunic, was shivering. 'You stay here,' he said. 'I can do the rest of this alone.'

'You can't go by yourself,' Curious said, flapping his paws in agitation. 'The crawly thing might get you.'

'He won't be alone, because I'm going with him,' Ned said.

'No!' Bess said sharply. 'Ye ain't going near that place again, boy!'

'I'll just go as far as the gateway, I won't go inside.'

Bess gazed at him in silence. The hob saw the look of indecision in her eyes. She wanted to keep Ned safe, but the chapman had to be taken to the abbey and she did not want the hob to go alone.

'I best come with ye then,' Bess said.

'Thank ye, but there's no need,' Ned said. 'We'll take the ghost as far as the abbey gate and we'll be home before ye know we're gone. And we've got the angel's feather, so we'll be safe, I promise.'

Bess shook her head and frowned. 'I don't know...'

Ned hugged her quickly. 'We'll be fine, Bess. To the gateway and no further.'

At last, with obvious reluctance, Bess nodded. 'Very well, but I ain't happy about this Ned. Mind ye don't go inside the abbey.'

'I *won't.*'

Bess looked at Jack Gaudy and the hob saw her shiver. 'This has been the strangest night,' she said softly. 'Ain't one we're likely to forget in a hurry.'

'Ye go back to the house,' Ned said to Curious, 'and hide behind the cupboard.'

'No, he can stay with me,' Bess said firmly. She smiled at the small hob. 'Ye both can, if ye like, when ye get back. Don't mind, do ye Ned? Ye can come and see them whenever ye want, and they won't be getting under yer mam's feet.'

A look of disappointment flashed across Ned's face. He looked at the hob. 'Is that what ye want?'

The hob hesitated. *I do not want to hurt the boy's feelings but I would very much like to stay in Bess's home.* 'I think so,' he said.

'Oh. That's fine, it really is,' Ned said with a quick smile. 'There're too many people in our house anyway.'

'It's settled then,' Bess said.

Curious held out his acorn. 'You take this, Brother Walter. It might help you against the crawly thing.'

It didn't help before, the hob thought, but he took the acorn and nodded. 'It might indeed. I'll keep it safe and bring it back to you.'

Bess opened her gate and Curious trailed wearily along the path to her door.

'Come home soon,' he called over his shoulder.

'I'll go and fetch Flit,' Ned said. 'We'll be home before anyone notices he's gone.'

Bess stood at her gate to watch them on their way.

The hob waited with Jack Gaudy on the green until Ned led Flit out of the yard. The boy winced at each ringing hoof fall. 'Walk a bit softer, Flit, afore ye wake my father. Don't want to have to try and explain where I'm goin' at this time of the morning. Come on, little hob, up into the saddle.'

As Ned climbed up behind the hob, he whispered, 'Look at the chapman.'

Sweet Cicely's curse was weakening by the moment. By now Jack Gaudy was straight backed and he no longer leaned on his stick. He looked years younger than he had at the Cold Fair and was gazing around with an air of bewilderment. 'Urchin..?' he whispered. 'Where are ye, girl?'

They set off for the abbey. The chapman glided along behind the horse. His legs moved as if he was walking, but his feet did not touch the ground. It was an unsettling sight.

They reached the abbey as the eastern sky turned from grey to gold. The chapman had faded almost to nothing and the hob was dismayed to realise that time was running out. If Jack Gaudy was not reunited with Urchin soon, then the chance to do so would be lost, maybe forever.

Chapter Seventeen

They stopped by the bridge near the abbey gatehouse. The hob climbed down from Flit's back. 'I will look for Urchin,' he said.

'I thought we were just leaving the chapman at the gate?' Ned said with a frown.

'The girl might not know he's here,' the hob said anxiously. 'I have to find her before he disappears altogether.'

Flit moved restlessly and blew through his nostrils in nervous little huffs. Ned dismounted and rubbed the horse's nose to try and calm him. 'Where's she likely to be?'

The hob thought for a moment. 'She likes the brother men's burial place. I think she might be buried there too.'

The chapman, now just a faint shadow in the growing light, said fretfully, 'Where's my li'l girl, my Urchin? Ye said she'd be here, waitin' for me.'

'Don't worry,' the hob said. 'I will find her.'

The hob ran across the bridge and along the gate passage. The chapman stayed close enough for the hob to feel the dead chill surrounding him. He stopped at the edge of the yard, looking around and listening for any sign of the crawling man, but silence hung over the empty buildings and nothing moved in the frozen stillness of the early dawn.

'What's the matter?' Ned called. 'Why've ye stopped?'

The hob shook his head. 'I'm just listening.'

'To what? I don't hear anythin'.'

'I'm listening in case there *is* something,' the hob said. He turned quickly at the sound of Flit's hooves on the bridge. Ned was coming after him.

'No!' the hob said. 'Go back! You promised Bess you would not go inside the abbey!'

'I ain't leaving ye to do this by yerself,' Ned said firmly, but there was a tremor in his voice. 'Sooner we find the girl, sooner we can go home.'

In spite of his misgivings about the boy setting foot inside the abbey, the hob was glad of Ned's company as he crossed the yard and hurried past the empty animal pens to the garden gate. The feeling that they were being watched riddled him with panic. He could imagine the crawly thing in a dark corner, biding its time, ready to spring. It took every bit of willpower the hob could muster not to turn and run back to the bridge. It was only Ned's steady courage that kept the worst of his fear at bay. The boy was terrified, it was there in his harsh breathing, but he and Flit did not falter. They followed him through the gate and along the path to the graveyard.

The hob could not see the girl at first but her voice carried on the still air and he knew she was close by.

'Sing for the king, the beggar, the fool,
Sing for the winter and welcome in Yule.'

Jack Gaudy gave an anguished groan. 'Urchin? My Johanna!' His ghost became clearer and the colours of his patched coat shimmered into view, vivdly bright against the frost-whitened graveyard.

The singing stopped abruptly. The hob saw a shimmer of blue through the branches of a scrubby hawthorn.

'*Pappy?*'

The chapman passed through the hob like a winter wind, making him gasp. Urchin started to cry as if her heart was breaking. She ran to her father and the chapman gathered her up in his arms and danced with her in slow circles. The girl's thin fingers twisted into the sleeves of his patched coat.

'Bin waitin' an' waitin' for ye, Pappy.' Her voice was faint and the hob could barely hear her.

'Couldn't find ye, girl. Din't know where ye were 'til this little creature told me.' He smiled at the hob over his daughter's head. 'If angels can be small and hairy, then that's what 'ee is.'

The hob's chest swelled with pride. *I'm not pretty,* he thought happily, *I'm a nangel.*

'Thank ye,' Urchin said. Light suffused her fragile form. It glowed from her eyes and surrounded her like the halo around a candle flame.

'Ye did it,' Ned said softly, 'ye really did it, Brother Walter.'

'*We* did it,' the hob said, a warm glow spreading through his body. Urchin was safe now.

'No! Behind ye, liddle Walter!' Urchin called sharply.

The hob spun on his heel and his heart seemed to stop. There, crouching in the long grass beneath the hawthorn tree and sniffing the air to catch their scent, was the crawling man. The blind eyes turned in their direction and the creature gathered itself together, ready to attack.

Ned cried out in terror. Flit whinnied and jerked the reins out of his hand. In a thunder of hoof beats, he was gone, galloping off through the gardens to disappear in the direction of the orchard. Ned tried to go after him but the crawling man lunged forward and grabbed his leg, pulling him off his feet. Ned yelled and kicked out at the thing but the crawling man was not going to be cheated of its prey a second time.

'Get away from here, Walter!' Ned shouted. 'Save yerself!'

The hob had no intention of abandoning the boy. With Urchin's screams ringing in his ears, he threw himself on the creature's back. Bones jutted through the rags and dug into him, as sharp as knife blades. With a hiss, the crawling man bucked and sent him tumbling head over heels across the ground. Jack Gaudy's furious ghost whirled around and through the crawling thing but he could do nothing to stop it.

The hob tried again, but the crawling man swatted him aside viciously and he lay winded for a few moments. He heard Ned's cries as the creature gripped his neck with skeletal fingers and lowered its head to bite him, its yellowing teeth grazing his cheek. Urchin, just a blur of blue and red, howled around the boy and the ghost like a winter storm, but the crawling man did not seem to notice.

Horrified, the hob managed to struggle to his feet. His whole body shook and he looked around desperately for something he could use to fight the crawling thing. A golden glint in the grass caught his eye. It was Curious's acorn. He had dropped it when the creature hit him. Snatching it up, and trusting that someone would be listening, the hob shouted, 'Help us! Please! Help us!'

Ned screamed and struggled to push the creature away but it was biting his hands and the hob saw blood. Urchin and her father raged and swirled around them, whipping the air into an icy frenzy.

'Help! Help us!' The hob cried out again. He clambered onto the crawling man's back, wrapping his arms around its neck, straining to pull it away from Ned. The purse holding the angel's feather brushed against the creature's withered skin and it screeched as if it had been burned. It loosened its grip on Ned just long enough for the boy to shove it aside and haul himself away. The crawling thing swung its bony arm at the hob, catching him in the chest and sending him flying. The hob landed heavily. It felt as if all his bones had snapped and pain burst inside him. He still held the acorn. 'Please,' he whimpered, 'help us...'

The hob was dimly aware of footsteps rasping across the icy ground. Urchin's anguished shrieks tailed away and her father fell silent.

The crawling man moaned, a terrible sound that sent shudders of horror through the hob's aching body. Slowly, he lifted his head to see what was happening. His dazed mind took in the green mist trailing along the path, and a pair of large hooves. The hob struggled to sit up, and he stared in awe at the tall, antlered figure silhouetted against the dawn sky.

'*The Deerman!*' he whispered in a trembling voice. 'He *heard* me!'

The crawling man cowered at the Deerman's feet, its withered arms over its head.

Ned stared up at the Deerman, his face white with terror. He held his bitten and bleeding hand against his chest and blood trickled down his cheek. The hob saw deep scratches and red weals on the boy's throat. Another few moments and the crawly man would have killed him. The Deerman had come to help them just in time.

On the path nearby, Jack Gaudy stood with his arm around Urchin's shoulders. The girl's eyes were wide and her face shone with joy as she gazed at the Deerman. 'See Pappy? 'Tis 'ee, come to dance us away...'

186

The hob slowly got to his feet, though his legs shook so badly they could barely hold him.

The Deerman looked down at the hob with eyes as dark as midwinter and leaned forward to lay a hand on his head. A feeling of peace slowed the hob's wildly beating heart and eased the pain in his battered body. Tears blurred his eyes as he gazed back at the creature and a deep sense of calm spread through him; nothing could ever be truly wrong in a world where the Deerman walked.

The crawling man dug its fingers into the grass and started to drag itself towards the brambles, a grey maggot of a thing, but the Deerman lifted his ivy and holly wrapped staff and pinned a trailing length of rag to the ground. The crawling man wailed and tried to push the staff away.

The hob watched in astonishment as the staff began to glow with a deep green light and the thing on the ground began to twist and hiss, shrinking in convulsive judders until all that was left was a pile of rags.

The Deerman looked down at Ned, cowering against the wattle fence of the graveyard. He bowed his antlered head to the boy in a slow and stately gesture, and then beckoned to him to follow as he walked away along the path to the yard.

The hob hurried over to kneel beside Ned. He touched the bite wound on the boy's cheek gently. 'You were very brave,' he said.

Ned tried to smile. 'Ye were braver.' He glanced anxiously at the Deerman. 'He wants us to follow him.'

'Then we'd better do so,' the hob said, helping him to his feet.

They walked along in silence, with Urchin and her father following close behind. Ned limped heavily, one hand on the hob's shoulder for support.

The hob noticed that the atmosphere had changed; sadness now hung over the abbey in place of the suffocating feeling of evil. Buildings where people no longer lived held loneliness inside their walls. With nobody to come and go and stir the air, it gathered in corners like cold puddles. The abandoned abbey was passing from the world, the hob realised unhappily. The stones would be taken and the buildings would be no more. He grieved for their loss, and for the days long past when he had been happy here.

The yard was empty when they reached it. For a moment, the hob feared that the Deerman had already gone back to the forest but then he saw the faint greenish vapour trailing through the kitchen doorway. He turned to Ned in sudden excitement. 'He wants us to follow him inside,' he said. 'And the treasure is still there, waiting for us.'

For the last time, the hob walked through the abbey kitchen to the cloister. The box of books lay where they had left it. Ned picked it up carefully with his uninjured hand and held it under his arm.

He glanced up at the roof and gasped. 'Brother Walter!' he called. 'Look!'

The hob peered up at the boss from where the Green Man had once watched the comings and goings in the alley. Now, in its place, a grotesque corpse creature, its face twisted with rage, stared down with blind stone eyes.

Ned and the hob looked at each other in astonishment.

'It's the crawlin' man, ain't it?'

The hob nodded and a wide smile spread across his face. 'The Deerman has trapped him up there. He will never be able to harm anyone again.'

'Pappy, I feel strange...' Urchin whispered. Her voice sounded far away. The hob saw that she was starting to fade. The chapman's ghost was just a patchwork of soft colours and little else.

The sound of pattering footsteps and scutterings came from the church. The hob ran to the door to the south aisle and stared in amazement at the strangest sight he had ever seen.

The Deerman walked slowly down the nave towards the great West Door. Behind him floated, flew or danced figures the hob recognised as the last few carvings and paintings from the abbey. An angel in white glided above a man whose body bristled with arrows, though they did not seem to trouble him. The angel's wings beat slowly, with a soft *whish, whish*. It held a long white feather and there was an arrow shaft protruding from its chest.

189

'The nangel painting from the chapter house,' the hob said softly to Ned, who had come to stand beside him. He pointed to a hare and hound, walking side by side, sniffing the air. 'They were in a roof boss.'

'*This* is what happened to all the carved stones?' Ned asked.

'The Deerman takes them all to the forest,' the hob said, nodding.

'Then what?'

The hob shrugged. 'Who knows?'

Two women, one in pale blue, the other in scarlet, with golden halos around their heads, danced in slow circles, laughing silently. A ram with fleece of gold trotted along behind them.

'*Oh*!' Urchin gasped. 'Look at '*ee*! Such a pretty beast!'

High overhead, a winged dragon the size of a horse glided in wide arcs through the nave. The dawn light glinted on copper-coloured scales and shone through its golden wings. It swooped low and skimmed the head of the ram, then twisted its lithe body around the angel, before soaring up and over the west wall of the church and into the dawn sky. Through the open West Door, the hob saw the dragon land on the church steps, its curved claws clinking on the stone.

Ned breathed out slowly. His eyes were wide and full of wonder. 'A *dragon*...wait till I tell Bess 'bout *this*!'

They watched the strange procession leave the church before hurrying after it, down the nave and out into the yard. The saw that the Deerman had reached the gatehouse. Behind him, standing by the garden gate, was the shadowy outline of a pig.

The hob ran across the yard, waving his arms. 'Wait! Please wait! You forgot the old pig!'

The Deerman turned his head to look at the hob.

'There,' the hob called breathlessly, pointing to Mary Magdalene. 'She wants to leave the abbey. Please take her with you.' He hurried over to the sow. She looked as filmy and fragile as a bubble and through her he could see the timbers of the gate. Closing his eyes, he reached out to touch her. She felt as solid as a living animal. He hugged her neck tightly. 'Goodbye, my old friend. I will miss you. But we *will* meet again one day, when the Deerman comes for me.'

She nuzzled him with her snout and grunted, then trotted away, ears flapping over her face, her large rump swaying. The Deerman waited for her to reach his side and then turned to Urchin and her father. He beckoned them forward.

Urchin wrapped soft cold arms around the hob. They had no more substance than river mist. 'I won't ever forget ye, Brother Walter,' she whispered.

Tears filled the hob's eyes as he watched Urchin and Jack Gaudy drift away across the yard. The Deerman lowered his head to

191

pass beneath the gatehouse arch. The freed creatures, ghosts and people followed him from the abbey. Ned and the hob followed them as far as the end of the bridge and watched as one by one, they reached the trees on the edge of the forest and faded into the shadows. Urchin turned to wave. Her blue dress shimmered one last time and then she was gone.

For a few moments, the hob felt desolate. He sniffed and blinked away his tears. He looked at Ned, cut and battered, holding the precious abbey treasure beneath his arm, and his heart filled with happiness. He thought about Curious, waiting at home with Bess, and knew it would be a long time yet before the Deerman came to take them to the forest. He nodded, satisfied with that.

Ned yawned loudly and lowered the box awkwardly to the ground. 'Ye guard this, I'll go and find Flit, and we'll go home. I don't know about ye, Brother Walter, but I could sleep for a week.'

The hob nodded. *But before that, perhaps Bess will have another bowl of pottage to spare*, he thought. First things first, after all.

'What will we do with the books?' Ned asked as he turned to go.

The hob smiled. There was only one place where they would be truly safe. 'We will give them to the boggart to guard. It will take good care of them.'

Ned grinned. 'That sounds like a fine idea.'

192

After Ned limped off to search for Flit, the hob sat on the box and gazed at the forest, sparkling in the dawn. It looked as if it had been carved from ice. He lifted his face to the sunlight and a feeling of contentment warmed his bones. The day would come when he would go back to the forest and find a burrow under a new tree, but for now, he had a home and a family, and that was more than he could ever have wished for.

CPSIA information can be obtained at www.ICGtesting.com
Printed in the USA
LVOW01s2133240315

431904LV00016B/307/P